PRAISE FOR NATHAN LESLIE & *THE TALL TALE OF TOMMY TWICE*

"Sure, the tale told tall by Tommy Twice is a laugh-riot, page after page of yuks, high-minded absurdity, and Ionesco-worthy wackiness. But beneath the gags and guffaws and gasps lies … that awful sense that connection, within a family or without, is downright impossible."

— Lee K. Abbott, *All Things, All at Once:*
New & Selected Stories

"Nathan Leslie writes with a superbly supple and balanced sensibility equally at home in light and darkness. His use of language is richly varied and invariably fits his characters and themes. His latest book is one more example of why he is one of the truly exciting writers of his generation."

— Novelist Richard Burgin,
founder and editor, *Boulevard*

"You'll want to read *Tommy Twice* twice: once for the sheer pleasure of the fantastic stories in Nathan Leslie's meta-fictional picaresque; a second time when it dawns on you that Leslie has to be Charles Dickens reincarnate—and *Tommy Twice* his post-modern revision of *David Copperfield*. Come to think of it, plan to read *Tommy Twice* three times. It's that good of a book."
— Steve Watkins, author of *What Comes After* and *Down Sand Mountain*, winner of the 2009 Golden Kite Award for Fiction

The ~~Terrifying~~

~~Terrific~~

~~Tantalizing~~

Tall Tale *of*

TOMMY
TWICE

The ~~Terrifying~~
~~Terrific~~
~~Tantalizing~~
Tall Tale *of*

TOMMY
TWICE

Nathan Leslie

An Atticus Trade Paperback Original

ATTICUS
BOOKS

Atticus Books LLC
http://atticusbooksonline.com

ISBN-13: 978-0-9840405-0-6
Library of Congress Control Number: 2012945080

Typeset in Euphorigenic and Caslon
by David McNamara / sunnyoutside

Cover design by Jamie Keenan

Pike's Peak

"Orphan." It's one of those antiquated words—like "vagabond" or "pauper" or "lackey." Outdated. Outmoded. But still—this is what I was. Still am. An orphan.

In the single, faded photograph I have of my biological parents they stand half in shade, half in sun. In a cracked driveway they lean against the green, wood-paneled station wagon. Spruce trunks frame each side of the photo. My mother wears a scarf around her head—a spiked paisley pattern, dollops like ragged paramecia. Her russet hair juts and curls from either side of the scarf. She's wearing a gray jacket with the collar up, high heels, and a skirt that brushes the tops of her knees. Stockings. Wide, thick-rimmed sunglasses.

The lower half of her body is cloaked by the shade, dividing her in two: I can barely see her feet. The slight smile affixed on my mother's face makes her seem bemused by the spectacle. The corner of her mouth lifts slightly, and her nose is wrinkled at the bridge as if she detects the smell of sulfur. I can see the sharp edge of her left incisor. I can't see her eyes at all, only the oval blackness of her sunglasses. She leans against the rear driver's side door of the car. Her right arm rests rigid by her side. Her left arm reaches out toward the photographer, as if she's waving, attempting to halt the action in progress.

My father is also cut in two by the shade, the lower half of his body darker than his torso. He wears white shoes: The glow of his feet penetrates the shadow. He also leans back against the car—his shoulder blades press into the driver's side window. He grins widely, showing off a set of lustrous white teeth. He also wears sunglasses, but with one hand he has lowered the glasses to the tip of his nose. My father is in the midst of peering over the top edge of the glasses, but the photograph catches him in mid-movement: Only the very top crescents of his eye-whites are visible. As a result, his arm is blurred. His other arm is akimbo, a thumb inserted in the belt buckle of his jeans. His hair is curly and unkempt and his mutton-chop sideburns plummet nearly down to his jaw line. A thick gold necklace loops over his v-necked T-shirt—a hummock of chest hair is visible under the semi-circle of precious metal. He looks ridiculous.

Aside from this photograph I don't possess a single memory of my parents. I don't *know* them.

My name is Tommy. My grandmother told me that my father's last name is, or was—Jackoby. But I've always gone by Tommy Twice. I invented it, thinking "Twice" would send off sparks, make the world stand at attention. I liked the sound of it, the ambiguity. I thought it made me seem mysterious.

Now that I'm grown I can, of course, look back on my childhood with a greater sense of perspective. I can see how odd it was, how different mine was than most. Unlike most of my friends, I didn't stay put. I was constantly on the move. But the most striking difference between me and other kids my age was that I simply didn't have parents. I tried to avoid the subject.

I suppose I came out all right in the end, though sometimes I'm not sure how.

My grandmother raised me, at least early on. She called me "Thomas," though she said she couldn't care less one way or another about my last name. My earliest reliable memories are of Gaga. I do remember a multitude of eyes watching me when I was very young. I do remember sitting on a rug somewhere, a plush red rug, eyes watching me stumble around drooling. I'm sure I picked up the name "Gaga" from one of these sets of eyes. The how's and why's are a muddle.

Still, in terms of early memories, it's really only my grandmother who matters. My mother's mother. Gaga.

Gaga raised me near the very top of Pike's Peak. Not the famous Pike's Peak. It was a different, less impressive one. Happened to have the same name. Elevation: 5,154 feet. The house that Gaga owned was a small rancher, balanced on the southern edge of a precipice overlooking a vast chasm. Up on Pike's Peak the echo was constant. Even inside our voices would reverberate: "Thom-a-a-a-a-a-s-s-s come-e-e-e-e get-t-t-t-t yo-o-o-o-o-u-r scrambled-d-d-d-d-d eggs-s-s-s-s-s-s-s."

Usually I couldn't see the chasm. I couldn't see down the mountain. The fog was an omnipresent blanket, seemingly containing a personality of its own. Especially early in the day, Gaga's house seemed to actually float in the clouds, released of its earthly moorings. Later in the day the fog would burn off and I could see for miles, but not before the fog swirled and danced and snaked its way around us, around the aspens and ponderosa pines, around the lichen-speckled rocks, around the road leading to Gaga's house.

In the winter it would snow so much on Pike's Peak we were often unable to see ten feet from the windows. During the winter sometimes we wouldn't leave the house for weeks. This didn't bother Gaga: The pantry and kitchen were somehow always fully stocked. Still, as a result of the fog and snow, I don't remember Gaga leaving the house in the winter before two in the afternoon.

Growing up surrounded by fog and echoes and barren rock was enough of an experience, but my grandmother also did all she could to ground me, to tether me to reality—her version of it. Gaga was a stern woman, to say the least. She was also physically intimidating: weighing in at over three hundred pounds and reaching over six feet. Everything about Gaga was oversized. Her teeth were the size of matchbooks. Her nose was the size of a pear. Her ears were like cinnamon buns. Her pupils were golf-balls. Her red hair sat crimped in a tight bun (I can't recall ever seeing her hair actually *down*). She possessed a booming voice that seemed to bore through walls and glide on the air for miles. Her face was stolid, rock-like, but also able to erupt into ferocity on a whim. If she grew angry, her already-large eyes would swell, her ears would twitch, her nose would flare. When angry, she reminded me of some fantastic deep-sea creature imagined by early nautical explorers.

But what I most remember about Gaga were her hands. Not only were her hands the size of oven mitts, they were rough, gnarly, calloused, affixed with yellowed fingernails that she ripped off with her teeth and stored in a clear mason jar in her bathroom. Gaga's hands pushed me, prodded me, guided me, grasped me, protected me. Gaga's hands were everywhere.

And they fed me. She fed me homemade applesauce. She fed me mashed spinach. She sliced hard boiled eggs for me, spooning the ovals into my mouth. She sliced bratwurst for me, spooning me each quarter-sized sliver. And every day Gaga nursed me, holding the tiny blue bottle of milk for me to suckle between two fingers.

Possessed of a quick temper—but stoic against misfortunes—Gaga began telling me stories, feeding me wisdom to accompany the nourishment. I remember her telling me stories about those she called "the waywards." The waywards were relatives who strayed, who fell into disrepute, who disrespected what should have been respected—those who were careless, or selfish, or overly concerned with things that Gaga thought didn't really matter. Mostly the waywards were men—uncles, cousins, brothers, her husband. Men.

One day she sat me in the highchair and pulled knobbed apples from a sack, peeling each one with a twist and flick of her strong right wrist. Odd apples. The warty fruit looked more like potatoes than apples. Gaga said they grew special on the mountain.

"Thomas, you always have to respect the law," she told me. Her voice boomed. "Remember that. Do you know what happens if you don't respect the law?"

I shook my head.

She pounded her fist into the flat slab of her other hand and glared at me to underscore the point.

"If you don't respect the law, you get what you deserve. Hear?"

I nodded.

She plunked a peeled apple down on the large, scarred cutting block that occupied the middle of the table. She chopped the apple in half, cored it, quartered it. She handed me sections to gnaw on. I had teeth and she wanted me to use them. Teething was for babies, she said, and once I reached the age of two she was done with nurturing. Nurturing was my mother's job, and Gaga was not my mother.

"It's time for you to become a man," she said.

Gaga told me of her Uncle Avery, a gambling addict who lost everything but his shirt, who died penniless. She told me of her twin cousins, Harvey and Harry, who turned to bank robbery—one was in jail, the other dead, a bullet through his skull. She told me of her womanizing brother, James, who became deathly ill with "a disease worthy of his crimes." I wasn't sure what that meant, but I gnawed on the corner of the apple wedge and drooled into my bib. Gaga even told me of Wayne, her hobo cousin—a drug addict—a derelict who traveled the trains, slept in filth. "Eats rats and maggots and pigeons," she spat, clubbing her gnarly fist on the table. "They all get what they deserve. They scorned the law."

I listened and nodded and drooled into my bib. I remember.

"Thomas, do you know what happens to disobedient children?" she asked me.

I didn't know what "disobedient" meant, but it sounded bad. I shook my head. Her eyes widened, sparked, popped. Her hands were clenched and contorted.

"The same exact thing," she rasped. "They get what they deserve."

Then Gaga stood up. She thumped out of the room and thumped back with a photo in a plain, oak frame. She slapped the frame down on the table in front of me. I was surprised the glass didn't crack. The black and white photo featured a gaunt man with a raggedy, uneven mustache and a bowler hat. The man stood back straight against a brick wall, unsmiling, peering past the camera. The saggy skin around his eyes made him seem sorrowful, pensive. He looked propped up, as if the last thing in the world he wanted to do was stand there having his picture taken. Even then I knew this was a man who limped through life, who barely made it through, if at all. I wondered if he was a wayward too.

"This is your grandfather," Gaga said. "*Was* your grandfather."

I felt a vinegary taste in my throat.

"He was a sap," Gaga said. "A weakling. Couldn't hack it." Gaga cleared her throat and her voice seemed, for a moment, to drift off. "Weakness is a kind of waywardness too." She told me her husband died ten years back. He was sickly, she said, because he didn't know how to take care of himself. He worked as a salesman, traveling up and down the coast, but she said he didn't possess a grain of common sense. I expected Gaga to say that he was a good man (or that he tried to be). I expected Gaga to say that she loved him, that she missed him. Nope. Instead, she told me she didn't ever want me to turn out like that.

"Thomas, you need to be tough in this world," she said. "You have to protect yourself. You have to fight. You have to learn how to scrape and claw. Otherwise, forget it. You'll end up coughing up blood in a hospital like my sap husband. I don't blame the germs. It was his fault. A personal failing. He didn't know what was what. He just wasn't *shrewd*. He exposed himself too much."

My grandmother snarled as she said this, the plum vein in her forehead pulsing, her hands in stumpy fists. Gaga stared at the photograph, then snapped it up from the table and hid it from view. When she thumped back into the room she didn't say a word. There was less thump in her step. She dropped her hands back into the sack of apples and peeled another one. Watching her, I remember hearing a single dry sniff as she held the apple. It wasn't much, but it was the only sign of mourning I ever witnessed from her. She was one hard woman.

I grew up frightened. Ready for the worst to happen. This was clearly a side effect of Gaga's intentions; she had it all planned out from the beginning. Plotted even.

But before I understood, I worked. As soon as I stopped wearing diapers I worked. Gaga had a seemingly endless itinerary of things to do around the house and in the yard—if you can call a craggy mountain summit a yard.

"Thomas, life *is* work," my grandmother said. "That's all there is to it. You have to work for everything you get. There are some kids who have everything handed to them. Don't you worry, they always get their comeuppance later on." I didn't know then what she meant, though I do now. To Gaga you had to earn everything in life. Everything.

Gaga put me on sweeping and dusting duty first. My grandmother didn't believe in the "new-fangled vacuum." Anyway, the flooring in her home was uncarpeted and she furnished it almost entirely in spare, Shaker style furniture. Likewise, Gaga didn't own a toaster or a television or a radio or a washer or dryer. "Don't have time for all that fancy gadgetry," she said.

So she showed me how to dust, how to sweep every nook and cranny, how to sweep the last bits of each pile into the dust pan, how to empty the dust pan into the trashcan to minimize any spilling. Once Gaga showed me how to do things, she expected immediate mastery. Nothing less was acceptable. She handed me a sack of rags, a broom, and a dust pan. I was three.

Now I'm here to tell you I did the best I could. "Good" to Gaga was a sucker's consolation. Gaga strove for absolute perfection. "Good" was not good enough. I swept every inch of the pine floor I could reach, but when Gaga found a dust bunny under her bed she went ballistic. I didn't know what a "ninny" or a "pathetic hunchback" were, but I knew they didn't sound good when she barked them at me. Gaga exhibited her love in a unique manner. When Gaga found a thin coating of dust on the top of the bookshelf in the living room, she spanked me with the prickly side of her brush. The fact that I couldn't reach this height was no excuse, she said. I needed to "find a way," to "make do," to "survive," to "endure."

Most of all she said I needed a "work ethic." I didn't know what that meant. I do now.

Aside from dusting and sweeping, Gaga essentially taught me how to do all the house chores inside and outside—how to mop the floor, how to clean the toilets, how to make the bed, how to wash clothes by hand, how to paint, how to spackle, how to wax the floors, how to change light bulbs, how to wipe out spider webs…I learned it all. Yes, I was scolded; I was spanked. The upside: I learned quickly. And the more practice I received, the more confidence I gained. If a three-year-old can have confidence, I had it.

Outside, Gaga was less picky, less stern. In retrospect, one of the reasons Gaga lived on top of Pike's Peak seems obvious: she simply didn't want to bother with the rest of the world. I learned later that she moved to Pike's Peak only after my grandfather died; this made sense. At any rate, she taught me how to how to split a log, how to mend a stone wall, how to pick up sticks, how to tend to a woodpile, how to shovel snow. The last part made up much of my work. The difference was that if I made a mistake outside she didn't seem to mind as much. It should be obvious where I preferred to be.

My least favorite chores, however, had to do with bodies—her body in particular. As I progressed from three to four, Gaga taught me hygiene—especially, how to take care of hers. Gaga first taught me how to scrub the flabby folds of skin on her back—the tough ones she couldn't reach. This involved a wire brush, soap, water. Once I mastered that, she taught me how to carefully rip the toenails from her toes: she said I could use my teeth, if I wanted. She also wanted to save these—in a separate mason jar. Gaga also had me shave her armpits, massage her calloused kneecaps, and clean behind her ears. I didn't know any better.

I grew up feeling like one of those parasite-eating birds in a symbiotic relationship with a hippo. I'm just happy I didn't have to pick her teeth clean with my tongue or clean her intimates. At least that I can remember.

Gaga fed me. Otherwise…I followed orders.

A Regular Ritual

I only clearly remember four times when I accompanied Gaga in her ancient boat-like blue Chevrolet away from Pike's Peak. Once was an ill-fated shopping trip to the closest town of Spencer. During this trip Gaga punched out a teenage clerk for what she called "insubordination." (She said the boy was "projecting an evil eye.") Then she verbally abused the store manager and found herself banned from the store for life. It was a good thing Gaga had most of her food (and clothes and supplies) delivered to Pike's Peak by her kindly neighbor, Mr. Brown—about the only neighbor with whom Gaga spoke. At least at that time. A widower, Mr. Brown was about the most agreeable man on earth when it came to putting up with Gaga, and later when I heard he'd died, I knew that Gaga wouldn't last long without him. Likely, only courtesy stopped Mr. Brown and Gaga from becoming more intimate. They were from a different era entirely.

The second trip from Pike's Peak took place when Gaga had to actually find a mechanic to fix the boat—the mechanic was the one person on Pike's Peak who didn't make house calls or cater to Gaga's needs. Gaga was grumpy that day: not only did she hate driving, but she hated *thinking* about driving even more. What she hated most of all were machines, their inevitable imperfections.

But the most memorable trip took place when Gaga drove me one autumn all the way down into the valley to pay a visit to the Crestview School. It was quite a long journey, and one that took me into unknown territory. As far as I knew the only trees that existed were aspens and pines, huckleberry and chokecherry farther down. I knew about lichen and rocks and moss. I had no idea any other surroundings existed, or could exist. I spent my early years isolated from radio and television. So I was, needless to say, shocked when we drove all the way down the mountain into the lushness of yellow hickories and red maples and pastures flush with creeks and wildflowers and houses and rolling hills and butterflies. I had never seen such colors. My grandmother's methodical driving allowed me to revel in the details. I knew then that I had to leave Pike's Peak no matter what. I was five.

The principal of the Crestview School was, however, much less interested in flowers and trees than the practicalities of my schooling. Bearded, muscular, imposing: wearing a red and black flannel shirt, he bore resemblance to a lumberjack, not a school principal. At his desk, he cracked his knuckles and wrinkled his wide brow and leaned forward. I could hear his pine chair creaking under his immensity. The wood under Gaga's immensity creaked back.

"What makes you think the very top of Pike's Peak is actually in this district?" the principal said. "Our busses don't go that far up the mountain, you know. You *know* how dangerous it is up there from November to May."

"Last time I checked this *is* a free country," Gaga spat, lips curling. "A child is guaranteed an education here by law."

The principal smiled, as if privy to a joke. He reached inside his desk and withdrew a pocket knife and a stick from a pine tree. He opened the knife and began whittling at the stick, the shavings curling out toward my grandmother.

"Ma'am. Law. You're going to talk to me about law now?" He creaked toward her. His breath smelled of hay and clover, as if he were a cud chewer.

"You're darn right I am," Gaga said. "You educate this child."

"I'm not sending a bus up there," the principal said. "You know how those roads are in the winter. It's a death trap. I'm sorry ma'am, but I have greater duties than to one child." He kept whittling, the shavings curling onto his desk, onto the floor. "And by the way, if you don't think there is legal precedent for this, you're dead wrong. I've been in this seat a long time. Pike's Peak is beyond our—"

Gaga stamped her feet and pounded her fists on the principal's desk in the name of duty, of American education, of liberty and justice for all. The principal stabbed the pocket knife into the wood of his desk, blinked, smiled, and said safety for his children trumped all that. In a way he was singing Gaga's own song (though Gaga would never admit it applied in this context). They eyeballed each other, veins popping, teeth gnashing. This went on for minutes. It was an old-fashioned stare down. When I thought they couldn't possibly stare any longer, they kept at it. Staring. Staring. Staring.

When, eventually, she could see he wasn't budging, Gaga grabbed my hand. Stomped me out of that building. Gaga was too shocked by what she called that "negligent nincompoop" to see any kernel of wisdom he might have. Gaga promised to call the county superintendent, to take the school system to court if needed. I tried to tell her it was fine, that it would be fine. She insisted that the principal was a criminal—and even worse, stupid. In the meantime, I enjoyed the scenery during the ride back home. It was all I could do.

Seasons changed. Winter walloped us as usual, and the house on Pike's Peak was soon an ice-encrusted fortress. Then the spring melt that year nearly washed the entire slope down the valley. Then summer. By this time Gaga had all but given up on the Crestview School. Though I didn't hear her barking on the phone myself (she only owned a phone out of sheer necessity), she told me that she'd had enough of "this bureaucracy crap." The years passed. I was turning five, and rules are rules, she said. "I guess I'll just have to send you off to school somewhere else."

As soon as Gaga said this my heart leapt and then sank and then leapt and sank again. I didn't know anything else other than Pike's Peak, and the thought of being away from it made me want to curl up in a corner (even though Gaga wouldn't have tolerated anything that self-pitying for a moment). I was fearful of the unknown—Gaga may have taught me how to face the world with a fist of steel, but she also taught me how to hide away in my shell. But on the other hand, the small glimpse of valley Gaga had given me left me with a hankering for something more than a rocky crag of a remote mountain. Even at the age of five I was perplexed.

"But before that can happen, Thomas, I have more to teach you," Gaga said.

The next day I received my fourth trip in the boat. This time Gaga instructed me to tie my sneakers tight, and then drove me down Pike's Peak. But this time she drove away from town on a dirt road that led out into the woods. As we made our way down the dirt road, Gaga suddenly pulled next to a lichen-stained boulder and lumbered around to the passenger side. She opened the door, unbuckled my seat belt and instructed me to get out of the car. I immediately thought I must be in trouble, that I must have done something wrong. I was ready to bend over and receive what was coming to me. Instead, Gaga handed me a thermos and a paper bag and walked back around to her side of the car. She maneuvered behind the wheel, slammed her door shut and shouted: "All right, now find your way back home." As Gaga made a U-turn in the brush and peeled off down the road, I could hear the pebbles ping against the underside of the car.

First I sat in the dirt road and bawled. I didn't care who heard me. Even if Gaga was somehow so enraged by my sobs that she turned around and thrashed me with a belt, at least I wouldn't be stranded alone in the middle of the woods. I didn't know where I was. I didn't know how long it would take me to get home. Worse, I was afraid: afraid of the animals; afraid it might rain; afraid I might get sick; afraid of strangers; afraid of the heat. Gaga had taught me to work; she had taught me how to be tough, but she hadn't taught me how to make do on my own. She was always *there* instructing me. Solitude was new.

When I finally pulled myself together, I realized that I didn't have much choice other than to use what I remembered to climb back up the mountain. I opened the thermos and saw that she had given me water. I opened the bag and saw that she had enclosed a peanut butter sandwich and an apple. She wasn't trying to kill me. This gave me hope. This made me feel I could at least survive for a few hours. So I began walking back. What else could I do?

Luckily for me, I didn't have to walk too far. By the time I had made it back to the main road up Pike's Peak, I saw Mrs. Duffin drive by—one of the neighbors. When she saw me walking along the side of the road she immediately stopped her car.

"What are you doing out here, Tommy?"

When I told her, *she* almost cried.

"Why, she must be the devil's own horny toad," Mrs. Duffin said. She had a way of talking like that. I didn't understand half of what she said, but Mrs. Duffin did everything she could to make me comfortable. She sat me right next to her in the big bucket seat, strapped me in, and turned the engine. I don't know if she could see my reddened eyes, but she asked me if I wanted to hear anything in particular on the radio. Since I had never heard the radio before, I had to first ask her, "Ma'm, what's a radio?"

Mrs. Duffin nearly gasped at that too: I came to the impression she was easily excitable. At any rate, she turned the radio on and I could barely believe what I heard. I was like a remote Pygmy never exposed to "civilized society." I was an alien from outer-space. I leaned toward the speaker on the side of the door and tapped upon it: my five-year-old mind actually thought somebody was in there playing the saxophone, drums, and bass. Mrs. Duffin laughed and kneaded the steering wheel and toyed with her hair. I could tell she wasn't looking forward to the prospect of facing my grandmother: I didn't blame her one bit.

Gaga actually smiled and rubbed my back after Mrs. Duffin left. She said that she didn't mind the embarrassment one bit. Mrs. Duffin didn't upbraid Gaga for mistreatment as Mrs. Hecht did later or as Mrs. Keeley did after that. I found out later that at least one of the neighbors did also contact the authorities. I was too young to know of all the behind-the-scenes machinations. And there were some.

"I'm proud of you, Thomas," Gaga said. "I didn't tell you *how* to get back home. I just told you to do it. Sometimes the best thing in the world is to make friends. You can't do *everything* on your own. Can't myself. Can't expect you to. You need to make do the best way you can." For Gaga this counted as a lavish display of emotion.

"Find-your-way-home" became a regular ritual. Though once I had to hike myself all the way back up the mountain, usually I was lucky enough to find a neighbor who held enough pity in their heart to drive me up Pike's Peak. In this way I made quite a few friends. I also never forgot to look at my surroundings again: I never knew when I might have to make my way back to where I belonged. I actually became quite good at finding my bearings, finding home. I learned.

By early September, Gaga had me shipped me off to Aunt Tess who she said would send me to a school decent enough to take me in. Gaga said she was on the phone all day trying to find a kind enough aunt to take me, and she settled with Tess; out of her daughters, Tess had the most "normal" household. I didn't know the whole story then, but I did know that Gaga was worn out. "I had five kids of my own," she told me once over my breakfast of plain wheat toast. She told me they never called. She told me they never visited. Her face looked puffier than usual, darker somehow. "Why I should have a sixth child as a result of your wayward parents is your own best guess," she said.

At Gaga's funeral, I stood in front of her grave and felt the wind gust against my back. Somehow she was always *in* the elements, even in death. She left nothing of herself behind. I didn't inherit a thing from my grandmother: she was far beyond that. We were all just happy she didn't burn her home on Pike's Peak down to the ground.

Oddly, Gaga left the house on Pike's Peak to my eldest cousin, a man by the name of Mickey Orlean. Gaga didn't offer an explanation for this in her will. She never explained it to me at all. She just wanted it done. A few years ago Mickey died, and the home was sold by his estate to a rich lawyer and his wife: they wanted to use the house as their summer vacation home. Now the house on Pike's Peak sits abandoned and overgrown for much of the year. I drove up there once when I was passing through the area, several years ago. It was foggy as usual, and I could hear the sound of my feet on the gravel echo down into the canyon. For a moment I forgot who I was.

A Long Trip

My last trip in my grandmother's blue boat of a car was the one we took down into Spencer. I thought she would just drop me at the bus station with a wad of cash and let me figure out how to get to Aunt Tess's house on my own, but instead Gaga took me by the hand and walked me up to the greasy counter. Then she bought the ticket. That was it for goodbyes.

I squirreled away in the back of the bus, behind an old man wearing a ripped, yellow rain slicker and a fishing cap (even though the weather was sunny), and across the aisle from a tall woman with a sun hat and a ratty beige dress who buried her nose in her immense flowered purse, sifting and shuffling through the contents. As the bus pulled out of the station, I waved to Gaga. She didn't wave back. She stood there with a fierce expression and stared at the wheels of the bus. Both feet on the ground. I wondered right then if I had made a mistake.

I didn't know how long the trip to Aunt Tess's house would take, so I kept my eyes peeled and I watched the road. My ticket read "Boomtown," but I didn't even know in which state Boomtown resided. I had to just wait and see. The blonde, baby-faced bus driver whistled along to the country radio station during the entire trip: though he looked like a kid himself, he seemed to know each and every tune. I can still hear those mournful dirges reverberate in some remote corner of my cortex. Since my grandmother didn't own a radio, I didn't mind the music one bit. This was all new to me.

We drove down the mountain and into the valley, past the elementary school which was, at that point in my life, as far as I had journeyed in the world. Then we followed the valley for some time, the mountains flanking us, the yellow and red and orange wildflowers blurring in the median, the elms and the shadows from the elms flashing by, the other cars zipping in front of us, smearing past. It was fast, fast, fast.

As we careened forward, the mountains diminished, thinned and flattened into the flanks of the foothills until they were only a green blotch on the horizon behind us, and then nothing at all. The land turned greener; it was lush and more houses emerged. We drove through towns with more buildings than I had ever seen—brick buildings, stone buildings, shops and sidewalks, and houses painted white and blue and yellow. Then the bus accelerated and the towns receded, and they became a blotch on the horizon behind us. I pressed my forehead against the window and stared. I took all of this in.

Soon we entered into a vast, flat land of green and yellow. We passed large square patches of corn and soybeans, rectangles of grass. The flat roads intersected, forming more squares, more rectangles. Geometrical. Occasionally trees stood out in the middle of the field, casting long shadows across the expanse of yellow. Cows and horses and sheep tramped through the muddy grass to small rivulets. Along rail fences the animals slogged through the flat, high meadows. The houses and barns and silos lay deep within the flatness, folded into the clusters of tree shadows, almost unobservable from the highway.

I thought that eventually the uniformity of the land would lull me to sleep. Instead, I was transfixed. The land was so different from what I was accustomed to when I lived with my grandmother on Pike's Peak. Each new mile was a revelation. I had seen a few horses and cows and sheep, but never so many at once. I had seen flatness, but never so much. Gaga had told me that Aunt Tess lived on a farm. I wondered if the farm would look like the ones I could see from the highway. I wondered what Aunt Tess was like. I wondered if she had animals, if she had children, if she was married. Other than the fact that she was my grandmother's daughter (and my mother's sister), I didn't know a thing about her.

At any rate, the man in front of me wearing the raincoat seemed to know something I didn't; as I thought about what the future might hold for me, the sky opened up upon us. I watched a sly smile emerge on his face. The clouds darkened and we drove into and through curtains of water. It rained for hours. I could still hear the bus driver whistle, but just barely, and only because he turned up the volume on the radio and whistled more loudly than before. Mostly I heard the sheesh-sheesh-sheesh-sheesh of windshield wipers. The woman with the sunhat clucked her mouth, and constricted it into a sour grimace, and then she snapped her purse shut. I wondered if she couldn't find what she was looking for, or if she was dismayed by the downpour, or both. She eyeballed the couple in front of her and then glared over toward me.

"You're awfully young to be sitting alone on a bus," she scolded, as if it were my fault.

I kept my cheek pressed to the glass and nodded.

"Do you need something to eat? I think I have a butter-scotch candy or two in my purse somewhere." She unclasped her purse again and began digging through it.

I shook my head and lifted my wrinkly paper bag. Inside the bag: A crusty peanut butter sandwich (the only kind of sandwich Gaga made) and a brown banana and an apple. Her fingers still deep within her purse, the woman smiled at me. I could see then that she was missing her left front tooth.

"Are you getting off at Boomtown?"

I nodded.

"Figured. I'm getting off in Misery myself. Been to Misery?"

I shook my head. I didn't think I was shy, but this strange woman I didn't know was making me feel that way. I told the woman that I was going to stay with my aunt, that I was going to school near my aunt's house. She told me that she was going to stay with her sister for a while.

"Well, not *with* her. But she's in town. I have a secret for you. I'm lonely," she said. The man in the raincoat in front of me turned his head at this. The couple in front of the woman shift-ed in their seats. The woman watched the couple. She watched the man. "I just need to get myself organized."

I didn't know what "organized" meant exactly, but I nodded anyway and crossed my hands on my lap. She went on to tell me that she'd lost her job, and that she was beginning to feel like an old maid even though she was only thirty. She felt as if she would never get married, so she thought she'd start over in Misery. She always wanted to live in a big town, she said. Not a city, just a big town. A town where she could meet a good man, a husband who would help her.

"Not take care of me necessarily," she said. "Just someone who will be a friend to me. A companion. I could use a companion, you know?" The woman's fingers looked stained, yellowed. Her hair looked dry, like straw. Her right arm was spotted with a cluster of red scabs. She scratched her ankles as she spoke.

At any rate, I was too young to know what much of this meant, and since I didn't even know my own parents, I didn't have much in the way of comparison. I reached my hand in the paper bag and offered the woman my apple. She took it, saying that she would split it with me. I nodded. She bit into the apple, spraying juice against the back of the seat in front of her. She didn't seem taken aback by the fact that the apple resembled a potato. Then she bit into the apple again and closed her eyes.

"This is the best apple I've ever tasted," she said. "Where did this come from?"

I told her it was from my grandmother. The woman nodded, took another bite of the apple, and then handed it back to me.

"Your turn," she said. She told me she was starting over. She said it was difficult, that life wasn't always easy. "I'm looking for work," she said. "And I'm gonna start over. It will be good." Later, the woman—Marta—gave me the phone number of the hotel where she was staying in Misery. Then she leaned her head against her immense purse, curled herself into a ball, and fell asleep on the unforgiving bus seat.

Corn

When the bus finally pulled into Boomtown that dark rainy evening, the only thing I knew for sure I should look for was red hair—Gaga told me that much about Aunt Tess. "You'll know her when you see her," my grandmother said. Otherwise, I didn't have my name around my neck. I wasn't wearing a special hat or outfit. The only thing that distinguished me from the rest of the other seven people who stepped off the bus into the Boomtown station was that I was the only child, the only five-year-old on his own.

It only took twenty feet of walking before I saw the woman I knew for sure to be Aunt Tess: the wild nest of red hair was unmistakable. Though her hair was as different from Gaga's tight bun as humanly possible, in hue at least, I could quickly see the genetic relation—mouth, eyebrows, forehead. But before I could register another thing, Aunt Tess ran across the black and white tiled floor of the bus station, hoisted me up to her shoulder, and circled me around and around. This was no easy feat: I was a lightweight, but I also carried a satchel on my back containing everything I owned (it was almost as heavy as I was). Aunt Tess whirled the whole kit and caboodle.

"Hey there, little Neph," she said. "You're just as cute as can be. Tommy! Little Neph Tommy."

Tess's outburst of enthusiasm almost made me wonder if she *was* really the daughter of my stern grandmother. I wouldn't wonder for long. When she spun me back to earth, Aunt Tess bent down to me and pointed over the bus station transom to the opposite curb along the Boomtown street. Following her finger, I saw a small white car glinting in the wet glow of the streetlamps.

"That there is your final ticket home," she said. "And I do want you to be at home here, just so you know. I'm into being up-front. You know what "up-front" means?" I shook my head. Just before we scampered to the car through the rain, Tess reached into her mountain of hair and withdrew an umbrella. Then she held it over both of us. In the light from the streetlamp I could see that her hair was a mountain, and that within this mountain things shifted and moved. I could see small wheels and food and animals scurrying in her hair. I could see handles and sacks and string. Pens. A broom handle. Bits of ribbon. A knife.

Aside from her immense cluster of hair, however, Tess was not nearly as over-sized as Gaga. Where my grandmother's face was seething with life, Tess's was affixed with her father's gentleness. Her eyes were deeply set, and her cheekbones angular. Her nose seemed a bit crooked, but not in an exaggerated manner. Her cheeks were dotted with sun freckles, and her forehead was creased and reddened by the sun. Her hands were small and slight, though her palms were dotted with calluses. I could tell right away that she was used to farm work.

Tess tossed my satchel in the trunk of the car and turned the ignition. Then she drove us down Boomtown's Main Street and pointed out buildings. "That's the bakery." "That's our town flower shop." "That's the bank." "That there—that's the movie theater. Have you ever seen a movie?" She knew enough about me. As a result of the darkness and the rain, I couldn't see as much as I wanted to, but Aunt Tess's enthusiasm made up for what I couldn't see. I asked her how far we lived from town, and Tess told me she journeyed there all the time. It's just a "hop, skip, and a jump," away from home, she said. Then Tess drove us out of town, away from the lights and the buildings, through pitch black darkness. I felt liberated—free of the constraints of Gaga's home.

During the drive to her house Tess asked me all kinds of questions about living with my grandmother. Was it too gloomy for me? (Sometimes.) Was Gaga too crotchety? (Yes.) Did we get along? (Mostly.) Did she make me work too much? (Yes.) Did I make friends up there? (No.) Then she asked me about my bus trip. Was it too long? (Yes.) Was it bumpy? (No.) Did I get enough to eat? (No.) I was overwhelmed. I didn't know where I was, and I just hoped that Tess could take care of me as well as Gaga did: my grandmother was about all I knew to that point.

At any rate, the last thing I remember of that evening was Tess describing the farm to me—the house, the land, her two boys, the dog. It was at that time that my body shut down: I crumpled into sleep. The next thing I knew my body was being lifted again—this time gently, through the cool night air, and inside. I don't remember a thing after that. My young body was spent.

I woke up with a beam of sunlight washing over me. I was sweltering. I lifted myself out of bed and I looked around. I was in a loft on the second floor, in a small bed to the right of two other small beds. The other two beds were messy—covers strewn at the foot of each, and clothes surrounding the frame itself. Next to each bed sat a bureau painted blue with puffy white clouds adorning the crest. My bed was also flanked by a bureau, but my bureau was red-capped with bolts of lightning shooting from an orange circular ball.

As I walked to the edge of the loft, I could see a vast room below me, also filled with sunshine. There was a kitchen near the far wall, a table, chairs, a fireplace, and large cushion-covered pieces of furniture which I had never seen before. Gaga only allowed wooden chairs in her home. A larger bed with bedposts sat underneath the floor of the loft, tucked back against the other wall. This home couldn't have possibly been any more different than my grandmother's. Where Gaga's house was broken-up and orderly and tidy, this one was airy, spacious, and cluttered. In one corner loitered a pile of cans and bottles and newspapers and string, all in a jumble. In another corner tools and crates and toys and coffee mugs, paint cans and bent curtain rods and clothes hangers and car tires. I immediately wanted to straighten. I wanted to clean.

So I climbed down the ladder to the room below and found toast and jam, eggs, and a bowl of pears. A note rested on the table: "Good morning, Neph. We're out by the coops. Help yourself to toast and hardboiled eggs. Milk's in the fridge. When you're done, come on out!" It was a good thing Gaga made me read so much; this was a lot to expect of a five-year-old. I guessed Tess had a pretty accurate idea of how I was raised. She knew I would be able to decipher her note, even if I didn't know what a "coop" was or what "hardboiled" meant.

I figured out the toaster. I figured out how to open the eggs. I poured myself some milk and drank it. An old black lab sat on a rug near the stove and two scraggly tabbies batted at each other by the door.

When I walked outside I saw the house was a converted barn. Painted in large white and black stripes, the barn-house wedged itself in between two giant oak trees. Some might be afraid to live with trees flanking their home like sentries, but most would be afraid to live in a wooden barn without insulation or heat other than what they could generate from the fireplace. Not Tess.

I found Aunt Tess under her mountain of red hair a few hundred yards away from the barn-house near the actual barn (this one stained brown), pouring chicken feed into a wheelbarrow. She shaded her eyes from the sun and waved to me, then bent down to my level and told me to come on over. She reached up into her hair and winked at me as she felt around for a moment. Then she pulled out a red baseball cap and slapped it on my head.

"We're in the midst of feeding the chickens. You want to come watch? You might as well, because you'll need to learn this."

She pushed the wheelbarrow of feed in front of her along the expanse of low-lying chicken structure. Every twenty feet there was a door. Tess pushed the wheelbarrow to the very last door and opened it. The first thing that hit me was the stink—I hadn't smelled chicken coops before. It smelled like a combination of rotten eggs and mud and shit, and I was immersed in it. Inside the building were the chickens themselves, clucking, cackling, shitting, bobbing, egg-producing chickens. Each chicken was penned in a hutch, each with a bowl of water and a bowl of chicken feed with an access hatch on the outside of the coop.

When I noticed this, Tess told me what we were up to: checking the feed for each chicken, and topping it off as much as we could with the kernels of yellow corn.

"The corn came from this land. It's all a cycle," Tess said. "We'll show you that a bit later on. For now I'll show you how to feed the chickens. This should be straight-forward. Then we'll show you how to do the water. How to do the eggs. Things like that."

Within an hour I was scooping the feed myself. Soon I was the one checking the feed levels. Tess was right: it wasn't difficult work. Especially with her there. If a feed bowl was cracked, Tess would reach up into her mound of hair, search around, and then hand me a new one. After removing the red hair—which Tess said might make its way down the gullet of a chicken—we were good to go.

Hose and Stump

After we had fed the chickens (Tess told me there were 323 total chickens), Tess said we should take a break. We went back to the barn-house, and Tess plopped ice cubes inside a glass and poured lemonade over it. I was wondering where her sons and her husband were. She kept saying "we." I wanted to know this "we."

"Excuse me for a second, Neph," Tess said. Tess withdrew a small black megaphone from her mass of hair, puffed on the mouthpiece a few times and bellowed: "Come on down now. Hey, Hose, Stump—time to meet your cousin. Repeat: come on down now for your cousin."

I wasn't intending to be rude; my hands covered my ears out of instinct. The sheer decibel level. Then she slipped the megaphone back into her red mountain of hair and poured herself a glass of lemonade. It seemed as if within her hair she possessed an infinite amount of tools and knick-knacks. I didn't know how this could be, but it was.

"One thing you need to understand right away—my sons are bums. Don't do a lick of work unless I threaten them with physical violence. One reason it's such a mess around here." I wondered how anybody could name their kids "Hose" and "Stump." Before I even met them I assumed they were stupid.

Suddenly I heard the sound of feet on the roof of the barn. I didn't think anybody could possibly be up on the roof. The barn was so tall, the roof so high, the pitch so severe. Then I heard a thumping sound of feet on the exterior walls of the barn, a quick burst down the face of the barn. Then silence.

Five seconds later two red-headed boys stood at the front door. They were both older than me—Hose was eight, tall and thin with long freckled arms and a small tangle of blonde hair that curled down to his shoulders. I realized his hair might one day rival his mother's. I noticed Hose had a tarnished earring pierced through the top of his left ear; he also smelled like cigarette smoke. Stump was seven, much shorter, squat, his mouth affixed with a mean smirk. His hair was also a mess, though since his head was so big it flattened around his ears. He was missing two of his left fingers. He kicked at one of the hissing cats.

"This is your cousin, Tommy. Tommy—my boys. Stump. Hose." Since they didn't move, Tess told them to shake my hand. They still didn't move.

"You boys don't shake your cousin's hand I'm getting out the hunting knife again."

They rolled their eyes and stuck out their pinkies for me to shake. I reached out with both hands and took a pinkie in each. They quickly withdrew their fingers.

"Can we go now?" Hose asked. "We caught two more this morning."

Tess nodded, sighed, nodded again. Then she sat me down at the kitchen table, yanked a handkerchief from her hair and dabbed her eyes with the corner of the cloth before she reinserted it into her hair. It was as if within that immense mass she knew exactly where the handkerchief belonged. Tess crossed her hands, looked me in the eye.

"You may have some troubles with them if you don't watch it," she said. "I want them to be my pride and joy, but they have a long way to go." Tess told me that her husband, Rusty, wasn't often home to help out with the childrearing. She told me he was a truck driver who only came home once every other month. Other than that, he was making deliveries. "But that's how we can afford to live here," Tess said.

I learned from Gaga how to listen, so that's what I did. I didn't have to say a word myself. I just let Tess do all the talking.

Tess told me that Stump and Hose didn't work because they didn't see their daddy work, that they didn't understand that he did something other than entertain them on the rare occasions when he came home, that they didn't understand that driving wasn't just for escape. "They think that he doesn't work. That he just plays. You know what they spend their time doing up there?"

I didn't know what to do. So I listened.

"One time Rusty built them a climbing rope that goes up the back of the house. They climb up there with a fishing net and catch swallows from the eaves where they nest. They sit on the corner of the barn roof and try to kill birds for a living." Tess told me that when they caught a bird they stepped on its wings and mashed its brains in with their boots and sometimes dropped it down to the ground level for the cats to gnaw on. "I let them because at least this way they are occupied. They love wringing a chicken's neck, but they'd never feed them. There's just something in these boys that loves to kill things." Aunt Tess told me that the school near town was a good one, but that she had some things she'd like to teach me. To get me ready. To keep her sons from pestering me too much.

Even as a young child, I could tell there was more to this than my aunt let on, that she had her own feelings at stake as well. She seemed worn and distraught about her sons in a way that was natural but that made her look older than she was. I felt protective of her right from the start. I wanted to see her happy.

That afternoon Tess walked me down the driveway that led to the barn-house, and toward the east where she grew twenty acres of corn. We ignored the cackles from Stump and Hose above us. We ignored the names they hurled down. She told me that she basically had to take care of the chickens and the corn all by herself. Rusty would help a bit when he was home, but as husband and wife they agreed that she would have the run of the land. I didn't know what "supplemental income" meant, but I quickly saw that it implied she did everything.

When we reached the edge of the corn field, she kneeled down, searched around in her hair, and pulled two grain sacks from deep inside her mound. She told me she never wanted to cut her hair—it always just seemed like cutting off part of her own body was something she shouldn't do.

"Oh, I almost forgot," Tess said, reaching back into her hair. She rooted around and withdrew a small pair of gloves and a larger pair of gloves and handed the smaller one to me. "This is so you don't slice your hands up on the corn stalks." The gloves smelled of vegetables—asparagus or broccoli, or something of the sort.

I nodded. Tess looked up at the barn and shook her head. I could tell she was thinking about something.

"No," she said. "I'm setting a bad example again. You wait right here." I could see her withdrawing the megaphone from her hair as she made haste toward the house-barn. Then I heard her hollering at her two sons to "get back down here and help with the chores."

Wielding the hunting knife, she marched Hose and Stump back to where I stood waiting. They each held a grain sack. They each knotted their faces into an angry scowl.

"Tommy can't reach all the ears you two can," she said. "You two stay where I can see you. Get to it." She poked Stump with the butt end of the knife and kicked Hose in the seat of his pants. They shuffled their feet, and as slowly as they could, they reached up and picked the ripe ears of corn, one by one.

If Gaga was there I knew Hose and Stump would face a corrective they couldn't ignore. I could just imagine her erupting into fits of fury, molding Hose and Stump to her will. Tess was different than her mother though: despite her outgoing nature she was sensitive, elusive, less inclined by nature to bark and shout. If she did bark and shout, it was merely to maintain the status quo. I could tell Tess was not a woman inclined to bend a boy over her knee and bring him into the fold. She was laissez faire—except when she couldn't afford to be.

So I picked as much corn that afternoon as a five-year-old could. And it didn't surprise me that I tripled the amount of corn that Hose and Stump picked together (but then again, they stomped on two mice and a garter snake). I tried to ignore the cobs they threw at me deep within the cornfield. I tried to ignore the fact that they held me down in the desiccated corn stalks and threatened to make me eat both the mice and the garter snake. I was just content to do my job, if they would only let me alone. I didn't want trouble.

"You know, you're making us look lazy," Hose growled. At this juncture I was pinned on my back in between corn stalks. I thought of the mangled swallows. It could have been worse.

"Yeah," Stump echoed. "We're not trying to do any more work than we already do." I didn't say a word. Silence, I guessed, would befuddle them. I was wrong: they shoved ears of corn and corn stalks and corn cobs down my shirt, down my pants. When they were through with me I was a scarecrow. I did slow down the pace. Still, since Stump and Hose completely stopped picking corn altogether it was difficult for me to *not* eclipse them by a wide margin.

At dinner that night—corn and potatoes and eggs—Hose and Stump sat across the table from me and glowered at me while Tess sang my praises. I had to eat the same food with which I was tortured earlier.

"Did you see how hard your cousin worked out there? I don't think I could pick that many ears of corn myself, and I'm three times as tall as Tommy. It looks like my sons have their work cut out for them, don't they?"

Though I was flattered—I always liked being "the good boy"—I also knew I would pay for the praise. I was caught between a rock and a hard place.

That night Stump held me down and Hose poured a pitcher of cold water over my head. I didn't scream. I didn't shout. I didn't tell. When they were through, I changed into dry clothes, piled towels on top of the soaked mattress and went back to sleep. I wasn't even in school yet and I was already prey.

A Lesson

I wasn't used to waking up at 4:30 in the morning, but I became used to it. For starters, the early morning was the one time I was guaranteed freedom from Stump and Hose. "Unless the bus driver is honking at the foot of the driveway, I can never get them out of bed," Tess sighed. "I've just about given up on that." The early mornings became our time. We would eat eggs and toast and drink orange juice and milk, and Tess would show me the ropes. The second day I was on Tess's farm happened to be a Friday, and Fridays were always what Tess would call a "meat and egg day"—when the guy in the truck would arrive at one in the afternoon. It was, Tess said, "a nice arrangement."

So I spent that morning helping Tess load hundreds of eggs into large plastic trays. It wasn't difficult work, but it was tiring and my aunt's lower back began throbbing after a few hours. Tess taught me how to place the eggs in the trays so they didn't break, how to stack the trays to make life easier on the wholesalers. Then that was that. Sitting on the bench near the chicken coops, we took a water break. It was late morning by this time and we could see Hose and Stump climbing back onto the roof of the barn-house, net in hand. Tess shook her head and tightened her left hand into a fist. For a moment I could see Gaga's fury in Tess's widened eyes. Her incisors looked sharp.

Suddenly she grabbed me by the hand.

"Let's go," she said.

Tess led me back to the chicken coops, still holding me by the hand. Her hair was bobbing with every movement. Quickly she opened the door to the first series of coops and her eyes darted at each chicken. "That one," she said, pointing to a chicken in the far corner. "Grab it." I lifted the cage and carried it out into the grass. Tess told me to drop the cage there, to just leave it in the grass. Then we did the same thing in the next room. From each set of coops she extracted one chicken, and I pulled the chicken's cage out into the grass. When we were finished we had twelve chickens clucking in the grass, each one an island.

Then Tess directed me to pick up each cage one by one and carry them to the barn. I did as she said, following her. Inside the barn was a back area penned off from the rest of the barn. We placed each cage there. The sawdust floor was stained, and white and black feathers wafted in the stale air of this room.

When we had the twelve chickens squawking in the saw-dust room, Tess told me to stay put. She said she would be right back. When she returned she carried a squat log, an axe, and a plastic sheet. When I saw the blood speckled on the plastic and smeared on the axe blade I understood why she didn't keep these in her hair. I also understood why we were there. It was meat and egg day, after all.

Tess handed me the plastic sheet, ripped a hole in it, and slid it over my head. She told me this was to keep me dry: I was going to be doing the holding, she said. I listened to the chickens clunk and claw at their cages. The sourness of the room seemed to increase. I could feel the tension, as if the chickens knew what was coming. I watched a feather gently blow along the sawdust and cling to a bloody streak on the wall.

"It's time to teach you a thing or two. Real life," Tess said. "The way things really work."

Tess plunked the stump in the middle of the room, sending up a poof of sawdust. I could see the bloody axe marks crisscrossed along the face of the chopping block. Tess popped one of the cages and lifted a white hen to her chest. The chicken's feet jutted out. Her head bobbed left and right, then lifted as she craned her neck to see around the killing room. Aunt Tess handed me the chicken and showed me how to hold the hen against my chest, pinning its wings beneath my arms. She told me blood is a part of this. I thought of Stump's missing fingers.

"You might also get flapped in the face, clawed. You'll be okay. This'll put hair on your chest, little Neph. Just make sure you release her as soon as I'm through. I can't be held responsible for what the chicken does when its head goes flying." I didn't know what she meant, but that lump in my throat returned. She told me that if I didn't hold the chicken well, she might only cut off part of its head. "There was that one chicken who had its head cut off and lived for weeks. Farmer fed the hen through its open gullet. We don't want that."

I held the hen tight, her neck resting against the cutting block.

"Sometimes, you know, I don't have the energy to manage my boys," Tess said. She spat into her hands and rubbed them on the axe handle. I could see her eyes widen, her face flush. She closed her left eye and peered at me as if down the barrel of a shotgun.

"I should have said something earlier: you've got to set a strong first impression with people. Fear is vital," she said.

Aunt Tess lifted the axe over her shoulder and eyed the hen. She bobbed the handle against her collar bone—once, twice, three times—and then suddenly let the axe swing.

As a grown man I've seen car accidents, muggings, I've witnessed psychological abuse. I once watched a man beat another man's face until it was mashed and unrecognizable—the jaw broken, an eye dangling out of its socket. But releasing that writhing, blood-spurting, shitting, pissing, flailing chicken that morning was enough to make me close my eyes and tap my shoes. At that moment I would have given everything to be back with my grandmother on Pike's Peak, sweeping her floors and scrubbing her mole-encrusted back in the tepid bathtub.

But then I opened my eyes. The chicken's head lay in the sawdust, blinking, staring up at me. The body ran around the killing room, flapping against the walls, blood spurting. The beak opened and closed, trying to make a sound. Finally the body slowed, quivered, shuddered, and collapsed in the corner, the talons clutching a clump of sawdust, bleeding into a soft puddle. As I grew older I thought about this image each time I ate a drumstick or sat down to chicken gumbo: the chickens didn't want to die for us.

Aunt Tess watched the hen to make sure she was done thrashing, then she lifted the axe back to her shoulder and peered at me again through her left eye.

"So, as I was saying, you need to take it to them. Don't let them push you around. Make a first impression."

I asked her how I could make a first impression when that moment was passed.

"Oh, you can *always* make another first impression," she said, her teeth gleaming. "It just has to be strong enough to wipe the other impression out."

Then Tess told me that when I went to school on Monday, I should punch the first kid that messes with me square in the nose, get him bleeding all over himself. Even if I'm suspended, she said, it will be worth it. I wouldn't have to concern myself with bullies from that point forward. The other kids would see *me* as the bully. Respect me.

"You *should* be a bully," she said. "It's not a bad thing to aim for." Tess bent over to the next cage and popped it open, grabbing the next hen with one hand. I took it from her, kneeling back into the sawdust again, pinning the hen to my chest like Tess showed me. When the axe dropped this time, I barely flinched. I was imagining my first day of school. Even more: I was imagining what I could do to Hose and Stump, what kind of pain I could inflict upon them to set the balance straight. I wanted revenge. I could tolerate cold water dousings and corn down the pants, but the more I heard Aunt Tess talk, the more I realized I didn't have to. I began to enjoy the sound of heads falling into sawdust, the thunk of the blade slicing through the chicken neck.

When Aunt Tess and I had run through all twelve chickens, Tess reached into her hair and withdrew a sack for the bodies and a smaller bag for the heads. We placed the sack of chickens by the eggs: the wholesaler would take care of the rest, pay her in cash. Tess showed me how to chop and grind the heads up and how to dig them into the soil for compost.

I don't know if it was the blood or the shit or the ground-up heads, but when Aunt Tess withdrew the broom handle from her hair and handed it to me, I didn't need her to tell me what to do. I marched up to the barn-house and sat at the base of the rope. When Stump and Hose clambered down the face for lunch, they didn't see me waiting there at the bottom. I gave them a fair chance to defend themselves. I let them put both feet on the ground.

Then I held the broom handle like Tess held the axe. When they stared at me, laughing and pointing at the blood and shit on me, that's when I swung. As hard as I could. I went for the knees first, smacking each of them across the knee caps. First I smashed Stump and then I smashed Hose. Their eyes bugged out and they crumbled. There I was, this little five-year-old shrimp, bringing them down with an old broom handle. Once I got them into the grass I used the butt of the handle, jabbing it into their stomach, into their ribs. Then I whacked them on the head and face until they had to use their hands to protect themselves.

For the remainder of my time staying with Aunt Tess, I didn't have another problem with either Stump or Hose. It took them a week to even look me in the eye again after the broom handle beating. They also began helping out more around the house, around the farm. I would give them a look out of one eye, just like Tess. They knew what that meant.

And on the first day of school, I punched Burt Bruck in the nose after he called me a "panty-waist." I wasn't sure what that meant, but I didn't forget what my aunt said. When the blood flowed in between the fingers cupped around Burt's nose, I knew I *was* a bully, someone to be respected. Not a bad thing to be in kindergarten, in a new school in Boomtown, USA.

Hair Warshing

About a month into the school year Aunt Tess decided she needed to wash her hair. Because Tess had actually never cut her hair, nobody knew how long it was—not even her. This goes without saying: it was a major ordeal for Tess to "warsh it." It was something she said she did only once or twice a year. "I usually just let it air out," she said.

This was a Sunday. It was a beautiful day, and the leaves in the large oaks were just beginning to turn. The air was warm and balmy. A delicate breeze wafted from the south. That morning even Stump and Hose were up for some early swallow catching. The four of us sat at the table eating fried egg sandwiches and corn fritters.

"Boys, I think we'll go down to the lake and warsh my hair. Whadda you say?"

Stump and Hose flinched and shrank back as if they had seen a ghost. I could imagine the machinations whirring inside their head. Their vivid fantasy of netting swallows and then crushing their heads under heel had, in one fell swoop, been suddenly shot down. What's more, I could tell from their reaction that this was a chore they particularly reviled. I remember thinking: well, it can't be so bad. It's just hair, and after all, my grandmother had me tending to her gnarly troll-like toe-nails. I thought: what can be so bad about hair?

Well, I found out that although Stump and Hose had the work ethic of a pile of bricks, they were smart enough to know when a chore was particularly odious and time-consuming and gruesome. Cleaning their mother's mountain of hair wasn't for the faint of heart or stomach.

The Steps to Cleaning Tess's Hair:

1. Emptying her hair of everything it possessed. This took three combs (each three feet in length with teeth the size of cucumbers), a shovel, and a rake.

2. Sorting the contents of Tess's hair. A partial list of what we found in Aunt Tess's mound of red hair included a tricycle, three frogs, an oven mitt, a hunting knife, a gun, four books, three magazines, two framed pictures, a fan, numerous pens and pencils, a paint brush, a hammer, numerous nails, a baseball cap, numerous bags of different types and materials, a lamp, a chain saw, flower bulbs, a calico kitten, a melted box of chocolates, seven phonograph albums, numerous eggs (some broken, some intact), numerous ears of corn, a dead chicken, a small pillow (the kind one would find on airplane), rubber bands, envelopes, a pink purse, an umbrella, curtains, a folding chair, a card table, crayons and numerous coloring books, a dead swallow, a fishing rod, and a net. We placed the animals (dead or alive) in one box, the household items in a second box, the tools in a third box, and miscellaneous items in a fourth box. Some items were too large to fit inside any box.

3.   Driving to the lake. Aunt Tess did this, while we collected any windblown items from Tess's hair. We had an extra box for windblown items.

4.   Undoing Tess's hair. Usually it was kept in a huge nest-like mound, but before we could help her wash her hair, we had to untie it. This was a job in and of itself. The knots in Tess's hair were confusing enough to bewitch a sailor, much less three young boys. Tess told us not to be afraid to use our teeth. I was tempted to use a knife or scissors, but I knew if I did that my days with my aunt would be numbered..

5.   Unleashing Tess's hair into the lake. The lake where we washed her hair was large enough to accommodate it, but once we untangled the hair, Stump and Hose took one half of the hair and I took the other half. They walked clockwise around the lake, draping Tess's hair in the water as they went. I walked counter-clockwise doing the same.

6.   We brought gallons of shampoo (the strongest available—usually reserved for circus animals), but before we could apply that to Aunt Tess's hair, we had to let the hair soak. During the soaking process, the animals in Tess's hair either sank or swam. On this particular day we saw insects, worms, spiders, mice, another kitten, and two baby birds scuttle and thrash in the water, then drown. Hose told me he saw a fish swim out of her hair, but I'm not sure I believed him. We always missed a few non-animate objects in the first step, and the tennis balls and staplers and bits of paper and cloth either sank or floated. We couldn't do much about them. Stump did collect a two-dollar bill once, which Tess allowed him to keep as a kind of tip. He promised to share with Hose and me, but I wasn't counting on it.

7. Then we doused her hair with shampoo, and massaged it in, circulating around her hair. Luckily the lake was remote enough that it was not populated with other swimmers, as it had been so polluted by Aunt Tess's shampoo in the past that the water was nearly pink to begin with.

8. Then we rinsed. This was a two-part process, in that we had to first "wet-rinse" the hair, using the natural wetness of the lake to shake the shampoo froth from Aunt Tess's hair. Then we had to "dry-rinse" Tess's hair by splashing bucket upon bucket of water upon Tess's hair, once she was out of the lake.

9. Drying. We brought fifteen blankets to do the job. Inevitably, the drying process was inseparable from the picking-dirt-and-bits-of-bark-and-sticks process out of Tess's hair: even though we lifted it and massaged it, my aunt's wet hair tended to drag on the ground. Stump and Hose showed me how to use some of the blankets as a shield against the dirt, by laying them on the ground and then draping the hair upon it. Still, sometimes the hair just seemed to have a life of its own.

10. Driving home. This helped speed up the drying, though it also blew shampoo residue and lake scum in our face. Since she couldn't bundle partially wet hair up into a mound, Aunt Tess was forced to allow her hair to blow outside of the windows. This was a distraction to other drivers, but there was little we could do about this, other than duck.

11. Once we got home, we had to reinsert the contents of all the boxes back into Tess's hair. Actually she did most of this work. She shouted, "There is an order to these things. You can't just stick them in anywhere."

We spent nearly the entire day warshing Aunt Tess's hair, and for our troubles Tess drove Hose, Stump, and me to town and bought us cheeseburgers and strawberry shakes at a local Boomtown restaurant. This was a welcome break from corn and eggs. Laying in bed that night, I asked Stump why his mother never cut her hair. Living life with such a mound of hair just seemed like a lot of trouble to go through.

"Ask her," Stump said. "She'll tell you."

"She'll give you the whole story if you're lucky," Hose said.

Until we warshed my aunt's hair, Stump and Hose were pretty much the same to me. In my mind I thought of them as one sack of nails. But, as usual, it was much easier to judge them from the outside than it was to understand what made them tick from the inside. I could usually understand Hose's personality by how he related to his father. Early in life Hose (and Stump, for that matter) worshipped his father, but this would change. I don't think Hose ever completely adjusted to the change. Later in life, Hose would spend time in the county prison for petty theft. He began to shoplift when he was seventeen, and by nineteen he was caught. When I paid him a visit he was twitchy and nervous and burning to hit the road, explore the world. Hose didn't go to college. He didn't finish high school. But he did try to make good in the world with a series of menial construction jobs. Hose tried to do the right thing. Still, as an adult Hose seemed to possess an irrepressible rage. This eventually landed him in a federal prison. I try to visit him once a year.

As he grew older, Stump's reaction to life, by all accounts, became more muted. He would withdraw, retreat inward. When he became an adolescent, Stump would try to counterbalance his brother's anger by being his mother's helper. While I lived with Aunt Tess, Stump and Hose were as tight as could be, later on they weren't. Hose saw Stump as a sellout, and Stump viewed Hose in some rough approximation of my early perception of them both. Stump wasn't the world's best student, but he graduated. He went to community college and finished that. Then he got a job as a bank teller, a job which he still has. He lives outside of Boomtown. His ex-wife moved away long ago. As he grew up, more and more Stump tried his best.

Rusty Returns

One night Aunt Tess received a late phone call as I stepped into my pajamas. Because we all slept essentially in the same room, we didn't have much privacy; Stump, Hose, and I could hear every word of the conversation. The good-for-nothings looked at each other as soon as the phone rang.

"It's Pops," they both said. I asked them how they knew and they said he's the only one who calls so late at night. "Pops is coming home!"

Aunt Tess bounced around the kitchen, a grin plastered on her face. She said the fact that her husband was coming home wiped out of her mind the fact that Stump and Hose had smashed one of the cats that afternoon with a sledgehammer.

"We can always get another cat," she said. "My hubby is coming home!"

Even Stump and Hose seemed excited, asking Tess when *exactly* he was coming home and predicting what he might bring them. Their tough edge seemed suddenly softened, limp. I knew by that point that my uncle was a trucker who only returned home erratically. But what I didn't know was how much the daily pattern of life would change when he *did* arrive.

The arrival happened first thing in the morning. I was just waking up when I heard the grumble of a large engine and even larger wheels churning their way up the driveway. The engine thrummed and thudded. It continued running for a few seconds, and then cut off. I could hear boots on the scraggly gravel outside the door.

Then he stood before us. At first I couldn't see him, since Tess and her tower of hair blocked my view. But then I could: my Uncle Rusty lifted Stump in one arm and Hose in the other and plopped them both on his shoulders. Stump and Hose yelped with joy. I was still in the loft at this point, watching. Rusty held a box to each of his sons and they ripped into the packages as if it were Christmas morning. Hose's box contained fireworks, and he grabbed the bottle rockets and cherry bombs in both fists and raised his arms above his head in triumph. Inside Stump's box was candy—all kinds of candy: jelly beans and licorice and jawbreakers and candy corn and hot tamales and sour apple rings and taffy and gumballs. He didn't have a box for me.

When Aunt Tess told me her husband was a trucker, I imagined a large man with a beard, a man who wore flannel shirts and smoked cigars and drank a bottle of whiskey every night. Regarding the booze I wasn't far off, but the rest of my imagined picture was just plain wrong. First of all, he wasn't tall, and he wasn't big, and he didn't wear a beard. Uncle Rusty topped out at about four foot eleven inches, but even through his leather jacket, I could see his taut muscles. And as I said, he was strong enough to lift both of his sons simultaneously. Later that day he told me he once bench-pressed a horse. I wasn't sure then what "bench-pressing" was, but to my mind, doing anything to budge a horse was impressive. Aside from his shortness (he joked that he was a "tall midget"), Uncle Rusty had speedy eyes, and a sharp tongue. He also wore a black visor—the kind card sharks wear. He rarely removed it from his head. His spiky hair jutted from his head through the visor in hard, stick-like spears. For some reason I thought of a guinea pig.

After everything settled down, Rusty slumped onto the floor and rubbed his eyes. He winked at me.

"I'm beat," he said. "Haven't slept in three days, maybe four."

"Okay kids, you heard him," Tess said, waving to Hose and Stump. "Go outside and play. You can see your father when he wakes up. Go on, scram." She looked up to me in the loft. "You too, darling," she said. "Let your Uncle Rusty get some shut-eye."

As I closed the door behind me, I could see Aunt Tess kicking up a rug from the floor and opening a hatch and leading Rusty down into it. Rusty was the first real male figure in my life, and there he was descending into a hole in the ground.

What was most surprising to me wasn't Rusty's exhaustion, or even Rusty himself—Aunt Tess had warned me. It was his children. Hose and Stump suddenly stopped slouching, stopped scowling, stopped complaining. They even stopped climbing onto the roof to net swallows. Instead, the first thing they did was run to the barn and fetch buckets of water and soap. They were going to warsh their father's eighteen wheeler.

I had mixed emotions. I was glad to see Hose and Stump straighten out and lend a helping hand. Still, *I* wasn't Rusty's son, and all I knew of my own father was the old photograph I kept in my satchel. That lump in my throat returned, and it didn't go away. I thought about helping Hose and Stump with the truck, but I just couldn't bring myself to do it. Instead I walked down to the chicken coops and checked on the feed (by then I knew how to do this myself). I could even push the wheelbarrow from the barn to the coops. I can still hear the feed shifting with each step.

Hose and Stump were laughing as they soaped up their father's truck, but that didn't stop me from collecting the eggs as well, or tending to the water. I didn't mind; I liked doing these farm chores, and since it was a Sunday I didn't have school to worry about. As Aunt Tess said, school is really just about going through the right motions. She told me she received mostly A's, and Tess said she rarely, if ever, did homework when she was a girl. I knew Hose and Stump never did homework either, but then it showed (they got mostly D's). They said their teachers didn't like them, and I thought this was probably true: their surly attitude and preoccupation with killing anything that moved didn't give a teacher much to like. But with their father home they were having a grand old time, *helping*. This must be what a father inspires, I thought.

By the afternoon I had completed all the farm chores myself, and I still hadn't seen Tess. Stump and Hose brought me a sandwich and then after quietly eating, they sat in the shade and *read*! When I asked them what they were doing, Stump put a finger to his lips and whispered: "Shhhhh, Papa's sleeping."

"How long is this going to last?" I whispered back.

"Usually as long as he hasn't slept. Probably two days, maybe three. All that lack-of-sleep gets backed up."

"Can we ever go back inside?"

"Yeah," Hose said. "We just have to tippy-toe everywhere. And you can't talk in there until he wakes up."

"That's stupid," I said. "What if I want to talk?" Suddenly, *I* was the surly one, and they were eager to please. A complete role reversal.

Hose told me that their father got grouchy if he was woken up from his sleep. Stump said that their father was even grouchy when he woke up of his own free will.

"And when he *does* wake up," Hose said. "You better watch out. He'll take us fishing later. He'll let us shoot off those fireworks. But first he's going to want to eat. He'll eat for a day straight."

"Nobody can eat that long," I said.

Stump glowered at me and asked where their mother was then. He caught me off-guard. How should I know? I said I thought she was inside, cleaning or something. But then I realized her car wasn't in the driveway.

"Nope, wrong answer," he said. "She's at the store. She'll come back with the entire car stuffed with food. She'll cook it all, and he'll eat every last bit. That's how hungry he gets when he first comes home."

I had to see this to believe it. I'd had a good look at him: their father was barely bigger than Stump. I thought Hose was lying through his teeth to make me feel bad about my own orphan status. Some kind of boastful exaggeration. But then I realized they might not even know I was an orphan exactly. So maybe they were lying just to lie. I wasn't sure, but I decided something wasn't right with this picture.

Aunt Tess and I had picked the last of the corn a few weeks back, so all that was left in the field were dry stalks. That's where I went to be by myself. I was beginning to like staying at Aunt Tess's house better when my uncle was off driving his truck up and down the country. Aside from feeling jealous that Stump and Hose knew their father when I didn't, I was beginning to sense that I didn't know what was going on any longer: I had completely lost the control I gained the day Aunt Tess gave me the courage to whack her sons with the broom until they couldn't walk for days.

Hose and Stump were right: when Aunt Tess returned from the store her entire car was stuffed with groceries. Immediately, Stump and Hose rushed to assist her. When I saw this, I bolted from the cornfield all the way up the driveway. I knew that I would have to lend a helping hand or be relegated to the status of who-is-that-scrawny-kid-anyway? But by the time I reached the car, Aunt Tess and her sons had it unloaded, and they quietly tippy-toed the food inside. I was the outsider.

"Thanks anyway, Neph," she said. "I've got to get cooking."

I was waiting for her to ask me if I would help her peel apples, or chop carrots, or boil potatoes—something. Instead, she brushed Stump and Hose and I back outside, saying something about "too many chefs spoiling the stew." I was confused—I didn't know we were preparing something to order. I tried to tell her that I fed the chickens and collected all the eggs already, but she turned her head as if she heard Rusty awakening in the hole under the floor. Then she put her vertical finger to her mouth and waved for me to go play in the corn fields.

The rest of the afternoon I did nothing but hang around the door and peek my head inside at regular enough intervals to see that Aunt Tess was cooking everything in the house. She was making soup, and lasagna, and pizza, and casseroles, and peeling potatoes, and baking bread, and peeling the skins from shrimp, and cracking eggs into bowls—all the time-consuming dishes which she rarely made for her children and her nephew. It was a sight. Stump whispered that his mother almost bought a *second* oven once just for the times when her husband returned from his trips.

When I went to sleep that night, Aunt Tess was still cooking—lifting casserole dishes from the oven, and unloading trays of cookies, and checking under lids. And when I woke up the next morning, still no sign of Uncle Rusty. Then Stump, Hose, and I were off to school. When we returned, still no Uncle Rusty. By this time, the entire kitchen counter was stacked with dishes. The refrigerator was bursting at the gills with bowls and trays of food. Everything was set up, ready.

To ease my boredom, Aunt Tess told Stump and Hose to take me down to the creek. I was shocked; I didn't even know there *was* a creek nearby. Hose and Stump were wearing their best clothes—the only clothes lacking holes or rips or stains I had ever seen them wear. Hose had even removed his earring for the occasion of spending time with his father. Tess's family had really built this event up to monumental proportions. It was as if the Pope were coming over for dinner. And for all intents and purposes, Rusty's role in their lives was ten times greater than any measly religious leader.

Stump and Hose walked me through fields of tall grass, for what seemed to be hours. I was in a grumpy mood. It was too hot for October, and I was growing impatient waiting for Uncle Rusty to come out of hibernation. The "creek" didn't help matters either—it was little more than the runoff from another farmer's irrigation pipes. If I closed my eyes and put my imagination into high-gear, *maybe* I could pretend the dripping water was a creek. Otherwise, though I hadn't spent that much time in my early childhood around bodies of water, anything I couldn't skip a rock over or at least wade into wasn't worth my time. I shrugged. They shrugged. Both Stump and Hose ran their hands under the water and then splashed a bit of the irrigation run-off on their respective faces. Then we turned back around. I was beginning to grow restless at the slow-paced farm life. I was only five but I was beginning to wonder if there wasn't more to life than cornfields, chickens, and rivulets of muddy water.

By the time we reached Aunt Tess's house again, however, I could sense a new energy—before we even walked through the doors, I had a feeling that Rusty was awake. And he was. Rusty stood hunched over the kitchen table, two plates and three bowls in front of him while his hands worked maniacally—shoveling soup into his mouth with one hand, and spearing steak with another hand. Then he dropped his spoon and used his left hand to pop shrimp into his mouth like peanuts. He must have swallowed them whole, because two seconds later he wrested broccoli and squash into his mouth, and then dropped his fork and grabbed two drumsticks, gnawing the meat from them faster than Stump, Hose, and I could fully step inside and close the door. Nobody said a word: we watched Rusty eat. Then we watched Rusty eat some more. And then we watched him eat even more. And then we watched him down a pitcher of water in under ten seconds.

All the while Aunt Tess stood nervously at attention, removing any unnecessary plates or utensils. She didn't bother reusing plates or bowls: before Rusty was done with one dish, she scooped and ladled and served him more. His hands were flying through the air, crumbs falling to the floor—a constant spray of debris. Tess skipped back and forth, her arms crisscrossing in her attempt to keep up with Rusty's ravenous hunger and thirst. There wasn't even a separation between dessert and entrée. Rusty ate everything at once, making little to no distinction between food types—meats and salads and cookies and pies and soups and bread were all victim to his gnashing, masticating, mashing teeth. I just hoped he didn't eat *me*. Barring that, I just hoped his appetite would soon be filled so the rest of us could at least munch on a carrot stick or a slice of bread—something.

These were relevant worries. Rusty kept stuffing his face the rest of the afternoon, in fact, and into the evening and the night. He ate for such a long period that by the time he stopped it was nearly time for us to go to bed. When Rusty finished eating, there were only a few hardboiled eggs and crackers left for Hose, Stump, and me. I could deal with this; at that point, I was just happy *I* wasn't the post-dinner snack.

But we only knew that Rusty was finished eating when he literally ate so much that his stomach split his pants. When I first saw him he was thin and short. After the meal, Rusty was still short, but he was bulbous and bloated as a snake who just swallowed a warthog. After wiping his mouth with a wad of paper towels, Rusty finally stood upright and burped. He smiled at his wife and walked over to kiss her head. Then he collapsed on the sofa and looked up at me.

"Who are you again?" he said. His face looked more bemused than annoyed, and he sighed. Aunt Tess told him and he nodded and told me and his sons to come down and sit with him for a bit. So we did. Tess brought us our eggs and crackers and a glass of water for each of us, and we sat with Rusty.

"Boy, that felt good," he said. Then he burped again. I'm not sure if I had heard a man burp loudly before, and I wasn't sure how to react. But when Hose and Stump looked at Rusty, I could tell we needed permission to speak around him. Rusty wielded the authority in this house, and nobody was going to challenge that even in the slightest way. He pulled his black visor down over his eyes, and he closed his eyes and sighed again. "Boy, that felt good," he said again.

Once we all had a little something to eat, Tess sat with us on the floor near Rusty's feet. Rusty's booted right foot was slightly swaying, so we knew he wasn't asleep. We could all hear his immense stomach digesting the poundage he had just ingested.

"Rusty," Tess said.

Uncle Rusty lifted his head but didn't open his eyes.

"Yeah," he said with a growl.

"Is there anything else I can get for you?"

Rusty's foot stopped swaying and began to bob instead.

"Nah," he said. He sighed. Farted. "Thank you. That scratched my itch."

I expected Hose and Stump to erupt into an explosion of "I did this," and "I did that." Instead, a whole new mood settled over the house: a carefully controlled one. For a moment I almost felt like I was back on Pike's Peak with Gaga. Tess quietly asked Rusty if he got enough sleep, and he nodded, then he lifted his head a bit more and said he thought he would sleep a bit more. Then we were silent as we waited to hear if he would say anything else on the subject.

"Dad?" Hose finally said.

"Yeah," Rusty said.

"We warshed your truck for you."

Rusty closed his eyes and clicked his tongue against his teeth and nodded so slightly I wasn't even sure if it was a nod. Then he said maybe it had been four days since he'd slept, and that maybe he'd like to sleep some more. Tess snapped at us to go to sleep, and she pulled a down pillow out of her hair and opened the hatch in the floor again and asked Rusty if he needed a fresh pillow. She walked on the tips of her toes, following him.

"Nah," he said. "I'll sleep fine."

That was the last we saw of him until the next afternoon when he woke up again, when poor Aunt Tess had to repeat the routine all over again.

A Tradeoff

One night long before I had met Uncle Rusty, Aunt Tess sat me down at the kitchen table and pointed at me like I had done something wrong. She stood at the edge of the kitchen, draping an arm over one of the chairs. Her other arm tapped her leg nervously.

"I don't ever want you drinking," she said.

I gulped and my skin started to get that itchy feeling it got when I felt ashamed, because I thought I must have done something to inspire the lecture. But drinking—I didn't understand. How was I supposed to get water in my stomach if I couldn't drink it?

"I can't drink anything?" I asked.

"Alcohol," she said. "Booze."

"What's that?"

She grinned at me and smiled as if she knew something I didn't—it was a smile laced with a twinge of pain. Spun the chair around and sat in it, placing her chin on the back of the chair.

"You'll know it when you see it. It's like the wind—you can always see the effects, the way it blows through people."

"Okay," I said.

"Let me ask you a question, little Neph," Tess said. "Why do you think this house is painted in black and white stripes?"

I thought that was a strange question, and I wasn't sure what to make of this little scene. I didn't know everything had to have a reason in life. So I didn't say anything at all. I just let her question dangle in the air.

"It's because of my husband," she said. "It's a kind of reminder of where he's been, what he's done."

I didn't understand that at the time, but when I saw Rusty after school the next day I thought about this little moment between my aunt and me. He was sitting at the kitchen table, right where he had sat the night before, engorging himself on every speck of food he could find. This time he was just drinking a glass of iced tea and leaning back in the chair. He had one of his boots propped up on the edge of the table. I didn't see Tess anywhere. He cocked his head at his boot and glanced at it as if he had never seen it before. He looked dazed and a bit muddled. Rusty didn't look up at me or Hose or Stump.

"Just the people I was looking for," he said.

I could feel the excitement pulse through my cousins—this is the moment they had been waiting for, probably since the last time he was home at some point before the bus swooped me into their home. I was beginning to understand the perspective of Stump and Hose. I was keyed up as well: I wanted to see what this Rusty character was all about.

"Drop your books and things and go on and hop in your mother's car. Let's go for a drive."

"Yes, sir," Hose said. Stump echoed. I just did as he asked without saying a word. Stump whispered that he knew where we were going, and Hose smiled.

When Uncle Rusty started the engine, he looked at me in the rearview mirror. Just at me. Stump sat in the front with Rusty and Hose in back with me. Unlike Tess, he didn't tell us to buckle up and we didn't. Rusty said he was going to take us somewhere, and that he knew we would like it. He said it wasn't far.

"I had some wild dreams the past few nights," Rusty said. "Dreams that seemed like they would never end." His voice was soft and reverent, as if he didn't want to scare the dreams away by talking about them. Maybe he felt that if he talked too loudly he would forget what swirled in his unconsciousness.

"I dreamed I was an insect of some sort. Some kind of flying insect in the desert, or on the plains. I would fly and hop around eating everything I could find. Fruit. Leaves. Dirt. Rocks. Other insects. Frogs. Fish. I bored myself into everything and ate it. I flew with others of my kind who did the same. They ate everything too. Then we began to consume each other. I ate my own kind. I ate my brothers, and sisters, and children. The dream seemed to last for days. I was the last one of my kind. That's when I woke up."

Rusty said that when he dreamed, he was always a flying insect, but that he wasn't always eating. Sometimes, he said, he dreamed he was climbing or swimming instead of just flying. In one dream, Rusty said he was the insect crawling up a gigantic rock. On the top of the rock was a lizard. Yet he continued to climb towards it.

"I wasn't afraid," Rusty said. "I saw the lizard with his lizard tongue lashing out, and I just kept on going toward him. In fact, I walked faster. This one was strange because I could have flown. I had wings, but I didn't fly. I didn't have any desire to fly at all. So I walked right to the lizard. When the lizard saw me, he cocked his head. He told me I shouldn't have come, and then his tongue lashed out of his mouth toward me."

When Rusty was done telling us about his dreams, we were already at the mouth of the cave. Well, I didn't know it was a cave yet, but that's what it was. It wasn't long until we pulled off Pasture Way onto a dirt road, and then we took that for a few minutes until it ended. Rusty stopped the car in front of a stand of trees. I hadn't seen that many trees since I came to stay with Aunt Tess, so I was surprised. There were thick older-looking trees and younger, thinner ones. There were trees I had never seen before. When I stepped out of the car it was shady and cool. I could hear water running.

Uncle Rusty walked through the trees toward the sound of the water. He didn't tell us to follow him, but we did. I could see he carried a black plastic bag in one of his hands. Once we passed through the curtain of trees, I could see that the trees followed the water. To our right was a thin creek—barely a trickle, but as we walked on, the creek became thicker and the water ran faster. The water ran muddy and I could see cobalt minnows swimming at the bottom near the russet pebbles.

We walked until we hit a culvert, and once we hit the culvert we stopped and walked away from the creek, up the embankment to the other side. The land was hillier here, different than everything else around it. When we climbed over the embankment we could see there was a rocky opening in it and the dirt and the moss and trees gave way to the opening of the hole.

Rusty reached into the plastic bag and handed each of us a flashlight and we turned them on. He flipped his flashlight on and pointed the beam into the darkness. We had to crawl a bit to get into the cave, but after a narrow entry it opened up into a larger room-like area, a few stalagmites near the far wall. It was cool and dank and clean.

"Well boys, this is it," Rusty said. He nodded to Stump and Hose and asked them if they remembered coming here. They said they did, even though it was years before.

"This is a man's place," Uncle Rusty said. "Since I have to leave first thing in the morning. Wanted this to be memorable at least. Can't do it all, but at least I can show you a thing or two." Rusty said it was important for a man to have a place to go to—somewhere that nobody else knew about. He said a man always needs his space. "Plus, you never know when you might have to run off," he said.

Rusty squatted in the cave, bouncing on the heel of his boots. Stump and Hose took that as their cue to sit down and let loose. At this point it was like Rusty had opened the gates for Stump and Hose because they both started talking at once. They began telling their father about the beginning of school, about the swallows they'd caught, about the trouble they were going to make now that they were getting bigger and stronger. They didn't say a word about the broomstick incident. As they talked I watched the flashlight beams dart and cross on the ceiling of the cave.

"Slow down, slow down," Rusty said. Rusty took their flashlights and stood them on their base so the beams shot against the ceiling in three yellow ovals. Stump and Hose clammed it. Then Rusty turned to me. "What's your name again, son?"

At this point I was the only one standing. I told him, and then he nodded and bit his lip. It was as if he were an old man remembering the detail from a past life. Considering how much he slept, I can understand the mix-up.

"Sit," he said. And I did. The floor of the cave was cold and damp. I wedged my flashlight in between my knees and aimed it onto the ceiling too. Mine looked like a moon in orbit around their sun. Uncle Rusty reached into his pocket and pulled out a small green canteen. He unscrewed the top, and I could see it dangled against the flank of the canteen by a small chain. I could smell something wafting from the canteen, though I didn't know at the time what it was. It smelled chemical—like paint or cleaning material. He took a swig from the canteen and licked his lips. Then he held the canteen to me.

"Drink," Rusty said. I remembered the conversation I had with Aunt Tess. I had a gut feeling, but I decided to ignore it. I knew, but I pretended I didn't.

I took the canteen and took just a sip. The liquid felt as if it were boring into my lips. Once my grandmother told me about the acid inside a stomach, how it could eat through wood. I thought maybe I was drinking Uncle Rusty's stomach acid. I spit onto the cave floor and Hose and Stump laughed. Rusty grinned and said, "That stuff is strong, right?" He passed the canteen to Hose and Stump. They were obviously used to the liquid, because they sucked it down greedily, holding the canteen to their respective mouths for a good five seconds each. No wonder Stump and Hose were so off-kilter.

"My sons like tequila," Rusty said, and screwed the top back on. Hose and Stump looked at each other and their heads suddenly seemed to wobble and roll on their shoulders. I could smell the tequila on their breath, on Rusty's breath. The whole cave reeked of it. That's what I remember.

Then I asked why they drank that stinky stuff. "It tastes like rotten garbage," I said.

"Sometimes in life there's a tradeoff," Uncle Rusty said. "Tequila may taste like roasted shit, but it has an upside. It makes you feel good." My tongue stuck in my throat. I had never heard a grownup cuss before.

Hose and Stump waved their hands above their eyes in the flashlight beams. They seemed transfixed by the movement.

"I'll tell you the same thing I told my sons when they were little tykes," Rusty said. "You've got to make your way in this world. And to do that you've got to do anything you can to get ahead." He paused and leaned forward, so that he could slide the canteen back into his front pocket. I noticed a quarter-sized rip in his jeans. They were also stained with blotches of oil. The heels of his boots ground into the rock as he talked.

I nodded and asked him what "get ahead" meant.

"To do well, kid. To do anything. You should lie, cheat, steal, maim, kick, scratch, claw. Kill. Life is a battle. Do anything you can, as long as you're careful. That's why I went to the can—I wasn't careful. I just didn't think things through. Still would have done it though. I had the twenty grand in my trunk. It was just that nosy security guard who had to ruin everything."

He stared straight ahead, then sat on the cave floor and stretched his feet in front of him. I was hanging on every word. I didn't know what to think of Uncle Rusty at this point, but I knew I was confused. My grandmother had told me I had to follow the law or else, and here was Rusty telling me the exact opposite. Aunt Tess had taught me how to fight, how to stick up for myself. How to be a bully. Then here Rusty was amplifying that even more. I didn't know what to believe, and I was too young still to figure it out. I had an intuition, a sense, but that's about all.

"A couple other things, kid." Rusty leaned toward me at this. Stump and Hose were giggling like girls at this point, rolling on the floor and play-wrestling. "We got to get you a game. And a weapon too. You need something to hold in your hands, just in case."

Rusty told me that in terms of games, a lot of guys have cards or billiards. Maybe cards. But he said his game was cro-quet. "It might sound pansy," Rusty said, "but when you knock your opponent's ball to kingdom come, well, I'll just say there ain't much that beats it. I'll play it right there at the truck stops. Nobody can touch me. You could have chess. You seem smart and that's a good game for a kid like you." He told me he'd teach me when we got back. Rusty pulled the canteen out of his pocket again and took another swig. He offered me more, but I shook my head. I was beginning to see why Aunt Tess told me to stay away from the stuff—it seemed to make people stupid, I thought.

"In terms of weapons," Rusty said. "I'm going to suggest a baseball bat. That's what I have. It's perfect because it makes a big impression. It will scare the shit out of a guy when he sees it. It's big. It's visible. And on top of anything, it's perfectly legal. An everyday item until you start swinging that bad boy around. In the rig I keep one right under my seat. We'll set you up, little man."

"Okay," I said.

"I could tell you about women too, but I'll save that for another day," he said.

When we got back home, Aunt Tess stood at the kitchen counter looking concerned but trying not to look concerned. Her eyes wrinkled. I could just tell Tess was worried in the way she held her back stiff as she chopped celery. Rusty kicked his boots off at the door and slid over to the counter, pressing into Tess and kissing her on the back of the neck. She asked where we had been and he looked back at his sons and me and winked.

"Just went for a little drive," he said. I watched Tess sniff the air. I could tell she knew about the drinking, but didn't say anything. That night we all ate in near-silence. I could tell Stump and Hose were depressed thinking about their father leaving again so soon. Then again, they also may have been coming off their tequila high. After dinner Rusty said we shouldn't be so mopey, and he asked Tess if she had any ice cream. When she dished out the ice cream, Rusty said it was time to play some games: cards, checkers, chess, whatever they had. He whispered to me that he'd show me how to swing a baseball bat later on. And that's the last I remember of Rusty's first trip home. We ate ice cream, played games, and stayed up past our bedtime. Mostly I remember him teaching me how to play chess—how the knight moves, how the bishop moves, how the queen moves.

He taught me openings. He taught me how to position my pieces so that my king is protected. At the same time, Rusty played cards with his sons, juggling two games at once.

Rusty forgot all about teaching me how to swing a baseball bat, though. I had to learn this by watching. As I went to sleep that night I could hear the bed creaking beneath us. Hose and Stump were out cold, but I could hear the moans and other things. I didn't even cover my ears.

In February Uncle Rusty finally came back. This was after missing Christmas and both of his son's birthdays in January. By this time Tess had cried and had a slew of phone arguments with Rusty. Hose and Stump rolled their eyes and Hose said their parents always fought. They seemed almost used to it. Tess called Rusty a "liar, a cheater, a scum ball" (none of which he would have minded). When speaking to her sons, she began calling Rusty "your father," as if she couldn't even bear to speak his name. Hose and Stump seemed beaten down by this: they stopped trying to catch swallows; they quit bullying at school; they were quiet. I almost felt sorry for them.

When he did return, Rusty acted as though nothing had changed. Knowing him, it wasn't an act. He just didn't care one way or another what people thought or felt—including his sons and his wife. He was going to do what he was going to do. But when Tess unpacked his bags and found the ball of pink and white flowered underpants tucked into one of the pockets, this was when the real trouble began.

"What the hell is this?" Tess kept saying, clutching the panties. "What the hell is this? What the hell is this?"

Tess wouldn't let go of the panties. She grasped them in her fist, as if they were a *part* of her husband, as if she would strangle Rusty by strangling the cloth of the panties. Her face was as red as her hair, and as she yelled and shook, bits of paper and toothpicks and rubber bands fell from her hair, as if fleeing for safety. Without a word, Rusty walked outside. I could hear his keys and a door slam. Fifteen seconds later he was back inside. He held a Louisville Slugger in his right hand. The bat was almost as big as he was, but his arm muscles swelled, and he thumped the bat back in his other hand and stood in front of Tess.

I thought Stump or Hose would do or say something to stop them. Even though I was young, I still regret my own inaction. We were all just shocked. Staring. Tess reached into her hair and pulled out the hunting knife. She held it in front of her, defensively, telling her husband he should stay back. Rusty never hit her. He never even tried to. But he hit just about everything else in the house. He decimated the table, the kitchen counters, the stove. He beat the bedposts: each one splintered and fell over. He whacked the sofa until it contorted and collapsed. He destroyed the coffee table in one swoop of the baseball bat.

Aside from the sounds of wood on wood, this took place in silence. I was hiding under my bed at this point. Stump and Hose stood on the stairs, mouths agape. But after he had destroyed everything he could destroy, Rusty dropped his arms and began walking towards Tess, bat still in hand. He held the bat so low to the ground it nearly dragged on the floor. I didn't see Tess lift her arm. I didn't see her lift the knife. But I did see her snap her wrist. I watched the knife rotate end over end. Then it was the animal howl of pain. Rusty slumped over. The clack of the bat hitting the wood floor.

As I grew older, secretly I always wanted to know what Stump and Hose saw. I'm not sure I trust my own memory of what happened next. I don't remember the puddles of blood, and I don't remember the ambulance. I don't even remember the hospital, the doctors, the operation. The only thing I can visualize is the knife hilt protruding from Rusty's knee. His stunned face. Then his body crumpling to the ground, the knife like a flagpole marking territory, a reminder.

I found out later the doctor consulted with Tess regarding whether or not they should remove the leg. The doctor apparently told Aunt Tess it could go either way, but Tess was certain removing the leg would be the best thing. When Rusty was unconscious Tess also told the doctor that a prosthetic leg wasn't necessary for her husband. She was sure he wouldn't like the idea. She said a wheelchair would be sufficient. It was only a mean-spirited rumor that Tess was having an affair with the doctor. I did hear they were childhood friends; I knew she was always wistful for that more innocent time in her life.

The Numbers Game

My Uncle Rusty received disability pay for some time, but it didn't pay the bills. Missing half a leg, he couldn't drive a truck anymore; he fell into a deep funk. It wasn't completely his wife's fault that he couldn't walk, but she was the one who jabbed the blade into his knee, so I expected him to seek his revenge upon her when she was wheeling him about or when she slept next to him. Instead, my uncle seemed so deflated about his missing right leg that he mostly wanted to sleep. My Aunt Tess wouldn't let him drink alcohol, so slipping into unconsciousness was his only escape. In retrospect the fact that they continued their relationship seems difficult to believe. Yet it was so.

By the time August came around, my aunt was so preoccupied with finances that sometimes she stayed up all night punching numbers into the calculator and drinking water by the gallon. It was a tense atmosphere.

Finally, because my Aunt Tess could no longer assure me that her family could support me along with my cousins, she suggested that I move in with Aunt Penny in the city. I had never met Penny, but at the time I was excited by the idea of living in the city. In my young life up to that point, I had never really been to a city. Tess said that her sister had four houses. This was difficult for me to believe. One day Tess put me on the phone and said Penny was on the other end. I didn't hear anything in the receiver. I thought maybe the phone was dead, but that dull buzzing sound wasn't there either. I said hello several more times, then handed the phone back to Aunt Tess.

"Sometimes she's shy," Tess said.

Not long after that, Tess loaded my few belongings into the trunk of her car and she told me she would drive me to the city. It was a Saturday morning. She said it would take about three hours, maybe four. I said goodbye to my cousins and, even though he was asleep, I shook Rusty's limp hand.

Then we were off. We drove away from the farm, away from the chickens and the corn and the barns. I watched them recede into the distance.

Aunt Tess didn't talk much at first. She said she was going to enjoy the quiet time away from her husband and sons. Tess said she wanted to just savor the drive.

"You're easy to be with, little Neph," she said. As we drove out onto the highway, she winked. There was always a portion of her personality that Tess left a mystery.

Looking back, I wonder if Tess was actually happier with her husband incapacitated in his wheelchair. Even if he couldn't help around the house, she knew exactly where he was at all times. It's not a generous thought. Still, I knew even then that the financial pressures had to make her life more difficult. I realize now she had a much more strenuous life than I had first imagined. Jabbing a knife into her husband's knee didn't help her, even if he deserved it.

I rolled down my window. Tess drove and turned on the radio. Then she turned up the volume. I could feel the beat, and the guitar pierced the air. The weather was hot and dry and sunny. In the mirror I could see hazy clouds behind us. But I didn't see a single cloud above the car or in the direction in which Tess pointed the car.

"This is the blues," she said. "What do you think?"

"I like it," I said. "It's good."

Tess drove us like this, thumping the butt of her hand against the steering wheel. She drove fast in the left lane, passing the sparse clusters of cars and trucks on the road. The cornfields were flat and dry, and the tar-speckled telephone poles whizzed by quickly. Soon the regularity of the telephone poles lulled me asleep. I dreamed I had to chop wood and pull the wood up a steep hill. I had to pile the wood into a pyramid inside a cart, and make it up the steep hill with the wood just so. Each time I tried to pull the wood up the hill, the pyramid of wood fell, and I had to pull the cart back to the bottom of the hill and start all over. Each time I tried to pull the wood up the hill again, the hill became slicker, more slippery, and I would fall back down the hill. The wood would tumble onto me. The wood would collapse in slow motion, and I would reach out for it.

When I woke up, I was alone. I was sweating. I sat up straight, rolled the window down more. The car was stopped, and I blinked from the brilliance of the sunlight. We were at a gas station. Aunt Tess leaned against a wall and held a phone to her ear underneath her mountain of red hair. I could hear her say "Tough luck," and "That's not my problem." The rest was muffled by the traffic and the sounds of people walking in and out of the service station convenience shop. I had a feeling she was talking to Rusty.

Aunt Tess tossed me a soda and I opened it. She opened one for herself and turned the ignition.

"I should have never married your uncle," she said. "You know, there were so many other nice men out there. Better men. Kinder, more considerate men." I didn't say anything to that. Tess turned the music up even louder and began humming along. She drove faster, slurping at her soda.

Eventually we made it to the city. The slow and muddy river appeared, as if out of nowhere. It paralleled the highway, and we saw boats on it, and kids fishing off bridges into it, and ducks and geese clustering around it. I liked watching these things. Then the factories appeared along the highway and in between the highway and the river. I had never seen such large buildings. I had never seen such smoke stacks. The air was different. Thicker, sooty. I coughed and Aunt Tess drove on.

Many more cars appeared left and right, and soon we were in the thick of traffic. I had never seen so many cars. Tess read a piece a paper and looked at a map and turned left and right and right and left. The sun was lower in the sky. There were stop lights. Blinking signs. Cars honked their horns. And of course I was in awe of the buildings, the metal and the glass. There were people everywhere, and everyone seemed to have a purpose. Everyone seemed to have something to do.

When my Aunt Tess pulled her car into an open space on a shady city street, I knew we had arrived. Tess looked at her piece of paper, then looked at the house numbers across the street. She nodded and tucked the paper into the seat.

"Well, we're here," she said.

"Okay," I said.

Tess brushed dust from my shoulders and turned me toward her. She cleared her throat and smoothed her right hand along the dashboard.

"Look," she said, grasping my elbow. "My sister is a little... she's different than me. She's one of the smartest people you'll meet, but she's...unique. Some people have a hard time believing we're related." Tess said she hadn't spoken to her sister in years, and that there was a good reason for that. They just didn't get along, and they hadn't ever since they were kids. Rivals.

"Okay," I said.

"Just do your work," Tess said. "Do what you're told, and you'll be fine. And don't forget what I taught you. You're a good kid. A unique child."

Tess wasn't much on physical affection, so when she gave me a hug I knew it meant something. Then she patted me on the back and said she'd stay in touch. She promised that. Tess stayed around long enough to watch me go to the door. I could feel Tess watching from inside the car as her sister opened the door and let me in. Then I could hear her car pull out and head down the street.

My Aunt Penny watched the car go, and she lifted her arm to wave. By then Tess was out of sight, behind the buildings and the cars parked along the curbs. Aunt Penny closed the door behind me. I could hear the click of the screen door closing on the outside of the house.

I suddenly felt like someone had scraped my insides out with a spoon. I didn't know this at the time, but in retrospect I'm sure I was exhausted by the upheaval. I was living with one relative or another when I should have been living with my mother and father—wherever they were...whoever they were. I just wanted to be a kid. Instead, I had to function as a little adult. All I wanted to do was eat dinner and sleep. I missed Aunt Tess already. I missed her mountain of red hair, helping with the chickens, picking corn. Even her rotten sons.

Aunt Penny silently guided me to an armchair in the living room. The thick curtains were drawn and I could barely see where I was going. The ceiling was so short, I felt I was back in the cave with Uncle Rusty watching him drink tequila. I dropped my bag at my feet and sat in the chair. Aunt Penny sat across the room from me in another chair. She hadn't said a word yet. I thought this was odd, but at the time my little body was too exhausted to care. I wasn't used to traveling.

"I'm Tommy," I said. I just wanted to get the introductions over with, get on to eating and sleeping. Aunt Penny didn't say anything and I could barely see her in the darkness. All I could pick out clearly were the rims of her glasses; the rest was all shadow and form. When I could tell she wasn't going to say anything, I asked her if I could use the bathroom. "I have to pee," I said. I learned from Aunt Tess not to be shy when I needed something. No response to that either. Nothing.

So I stood up and felt my way around the corner to the bathroom, and I turned on the light. The tiny room was painted bright red—the loudest, most garish red you can possibly imagine. And the bathroom was so tiny I couldn't understand how they fit the toilet through the door. In fact, the door itself looked less like a door than an ironing board flipped upright. I was a young child and I nearly had to stand sideways to do my business.

When I left the bathroom, I looked the other way around the corner. Along the far wall—if you can call it far—one of the curtains was cracked, leaving me enough light to see. At this point the sun was setting. The kitchen was tiny, maybe five feet wide and six feet deep. Beyond that was a thin staircase. As a result of both the narrowness and the short ceiling, I didn't see how any full-grown adult could make their way up the stairs. I walked back to the living room and Aunt Penny was still sitting on the chair, staring at me. When my vision adjusted, I could see the whites of her eyes. I could see her arms were flat by her side. Her feet were both flat on the rug. The living room was tiny too—only big enough for two armchairs and a door to the outside.

We sat in silence. I wasn't sure what was going on. I wasn't sure why Aunt Penny wasn't talking, why she wasn't busy imbuing me with her wisdom. Aunt Tess had said she was smart, but I didn't even know if she could *talk* yet. I thought maybe she had injured her tongue. I thought maybe she didn't like boys. But eventually, when the room was completely dark, I heard

Aunt Penny stand up. I felt her walk by me in a crouch, ducking her head under the ceiling, and walk into the kitchen. Then I heard a click and there was light. I followed the light into the kitchen.

Aunt Penny didn't exactly smile, but she didn't frown either. Penny was thin: that's the first thing I remember noticing. She was so thin, so very pale. I felt as if I could see *through* her face. Her body was covered by a long cardigan sweater, with small black buttons. The sweater was dotted with white and gray lint. She wore a long skirt underneath the sweater that draped down to her ankles. Penny's feet were covered by slippers that must have once been white but had turned gray from overuse. I also noticed her hair wasn't red; her hair was brown. She pointed to the bench at the edge of the counter, and I took that as a sign I should sit. So I did. Penny closed her eyes, then she blinked them open. The kitchen was painted in the same bright red as the bathroom. Because of this, the counters seemed even whiter than they probably were.

"Hello, Tommy," she said.

"Hi," I said.

"Explanation: I usually don't speak in the summer when the sun is up," she said. "I also don't talk when I eat." This is the way Penny was. Just the facts. She didn't see a need for niceties. I could hear my grandmother's voice in her. Then Penny turned away from me and opened a small refrigerator set into the wall above the stone. She pulled out a container, opened it, and she poured the contents of the container into a pot on the stove and turned on the gas to heat it. I watched her every move. I wasn't sure what to make of Penny, but I was fascinated. She handed me a plate of crackers surrounded by circular cheese slices. She handed me a glass of water. In the silence, I could hear each and every move my aunt made. I realized how loud Aunt Tess's house was in comparison: all that noise from her sons. There was a constant ruckus. At Penny's house—utter stillness.

When the soup was steaming, Penny ladled out a bowl to me and handed me a spoon. She ladled a bowl of soup for herself, then opened a small closet and pulled out another bench, placed it on the kitchen floor and sat on it. Tess had told me that Penny was her younger sister, but she looked older. Her eyes were more widely spaced. Penny's face wasn't wrinkly, but it was angular, and her eyes just seemed further away. Maybe it was also the pensive silence that made her seem more of a grown-up—more like my grandmother than Tess.

To that point in my life, the bowl of soup was the most delicious meal I had ever eaten. The broth was somehow both salty and sweet, and chock-filled with meats and tasty vegetables and herbs I didn't even know the names of yet—artichokes, squash, olives, basil, oregano. As we ate in silence, I looked around the room. The first thing I noticed was an enormous calendar on the inside wall of the tiny staircase. The calendar was covered with scribbles in black and red ink. I gobbled up the crackers and cheese and slurped the soup. When I finished, Aunt Penny was barely beginning. I would learn later that she believed in chewing each bite of food twenty seven times exactly—even soup.

After we ate, Penny sighed and removed her glasses. She rubbed her eyes and placed her glasses back on the ledge of her nose. Then she spoke. Penny said she had already enrolled me

in the local school, and that I would begin my education tomorrow. I was shocked at this, because it was still August. But I had
no choice other than to believe what my aunt said. She said that
since I was probably going to need to sleep, I could bed down
in the attic. "I own a fan," she said. The way she spoke seemed
so strange to me. "I don't see the need for it," she said. "I don't
sleep much."

Aunt Penny stooped and brought my bags upstairs to the
attic for me. I was surprised Penny's tiny house even had an
attic, but really it wasn't much more than a crawl-space. I was
small, and even I couldn't stand up fully without conking my
head. The bed looked like something out of a dollhouse, and it
was only covered by a single sheet and a pillow. Penny opened
the small window and turned on the fan, and it felt good in the
stuffiness of the attic.

Going up to the attic I couldn't help but notice the gigantic
picture hanging above Penny's bed. It was a photo of a man's
face. The man was wearing a cap and the clouds behind his head
were so white they seemed to give off a glow. A triangle of blue
sky floated in one corner of the photo. There was barely enough
space in Penny's room for the immense photo and the bed. The
man smiled into the camera, as if he were ready to tell a joke.
His eyes were huge, the size of tennis balls. This was all she
needed, all she wanted.

Away

It took me a month to come up with the nerve to ask Aunt Penny who the man in the photo was. It was night and Penny was sitting in her armchair. The one lamp in the room glowed—only because I had turned it on. We had already eaten.

When Penny heard my question she gave me a look that was half none-of-your-business, half desolation. Then she told me: "That's my husband," she said.

I asked her if he was dead. This wouldn't have surprised me. She didn't seem shocked by the question. No, she said, he was alive. "Away." I asked her where—I was born curious. She made a circle with her finger, and then pointed to a spot on the invisible globe in front of her. "Right there," she said. She said he always came back for the holidays. "We have a house for that," she said. "We'll have to figure out what to do with you then."

I definitely didn't like the sound of that, but since I was just a pipsqueak and she was talking about December, I didn't want to worry about it. As far as I was concerned, December was a lifetime away.

School was enough to occupy my thoughts. As Tess had taught me, I punched a kid out on my first day of school. Blood spurted all over the cafeteria floor, and the vice principal handed me an in-school suspension (a light punishment, only given to new kids he was trying to "integrate" into the school). I quickly became the bully of first grade: nobody bothered me. I also didn't make any friends. What surprised me was the school wasn't that different from the one in the country. There were more kids, and different types of kids. Otherwise, it just seemed like the same thing: we read, we practiced our writing, we added, we made things with construction paper and played outside and ate lunch and read and wrote and added some more. Then we came home.

But when I did come home from school Aunt Penny would be sitting in her armchair in the dark with the curtains drawn. Eyes closed. She always had her arms by her side, though I could tell by the way she breathed that she wasn't asleep. Often she didn't bathe. I also came to realize she always wore the same cardigan—winter, spring, summer, and fall. I didn't understand what she was doing and I didn't have the language then to ask her. I didn't know what to say, what to do.

When Aunt Tess called to ask me how I was doing, I told her in a whisper what Penny did, and Tess told me to just ask her why she sat in the chair. Tess said Penny would tell me. Penny had "very strong beliefs," Tess said. I wasn't sure what that meant, but I wanted to find out.

After dinner one night I summoned the courage to ask her. This time Penny was sitting in her arm chair, holding her hands together. Her feet were flat on the floor still, and she barely moved. Even my crippled Uncle Rusty got around more than my Aunt Penny. So I asked Penny in the same way as I asked her about the gigantic photograph.

"Aunt Penny," I said. "Can I ask you something?"

When she nodded I went on to the second part of my question—the real meat and guts of it.

"Aunt Penny, why do you sit in your chair so much?"

Penny closed her eyes for a moment and then she opened them.

"Like to," she said. And immediately I thought Aunt Tess might be wrong about her sister. Maybe, I thought, Aunt Tess hadn't talked to her sister in so long she no longer knew what Penny was really like. But then Penny swallowed and licked her top lip ever-so-slightly. "I also am in the middle of a project," she said. Penny was like this—quiet and ambiguous. She figured time would reveal what it needed to.

I told her I wasn't sure I understood, but Penny didn't seem frustrated by this or tired of my questions. I just felt lucky, as if I'd caught her at a good time. Penny told me that her life was different than most people's—she was sure of that. She said she knew she might seem odd or strange to some. This was more emotion than I had gotten out of Penny in all the weeks leading up to my prying. She spoke slowly, clearly.

"My husband always wanted to travel. See the world. Wanted to be a part of the military. So here I am. Alone. Like my mother. Like your grandmother. Two ways of handling all this time, I realized. I could sulk; I could be unhappy. Or I could make do. I could learn how to live without." Since I was so young, I probably didn't know the meaning of some of the words she used. But I could tell she was serious. I knew she had reasons.

"Became an artist," she said. "That's what I am. I make thoughts. I'm not just sitting here staring at the wall. I'm creating things with my thoughts."

Penny told me she mostly created shapes with her thoughts—the kind of complicated shapes that could never exist in the world. She also said she visited other planets in her mind. Sometimes she became so immersed in this, she said she wasn't sure where she was. Penny said that she could close her eyes, and in a matter of moments, she could feel herself on the surface of a distant planet. She said she had friends on other planets—friends she often visited.

As a child I knew this was odd, that what she said was unusual. But I didn't know the extent of it. I had no concept of how *systematic* my aunt was. I knew that the calendar was decorated with symbols and numbers. Still, I could only arrive at a hint of the loneliness. Because she said she had a way of managing, I believed her.

The next day, after dinner, Penny sat in her usual chair and continued talking, as if our conversation hadn't stopped for sleep, for school, for everything else that occurred in the last twenty four hours.

"And I talk to my husband this way," she said. "That's also true."

I thought she meant over the phone—she wasn't always clear. Actually, I wasn't sure what she meant at all. So I asked her: I was becoming more brave.

"No, by sitting here. This way. I'm talking to him right now," she said. She paused, closed her eyes, and then opened them. "Okay, I'm done."

But when I asked her how they talked without talking, she didn't say. When I asked Penny where he was, she just went through the same old explanation. For the first time, I was beginning to feel as if an adult was lying to me. She did always know what I was thinking and feeling. I couldn't explain it.

Neither could Penny when I asked her. "I can't put it into words. Can't explain it," she said.

Eventually I did become friends with several boys in my first-grade class—the boys who weren't afraid of me. Kenny, Brian, and David. They were normal kids with normal homes. Parents. Dogs. During the weekends I began to go over to Kenny's house to play. Then to Brian's. Then to David's. Their parents would pick me up. I would meet them in front of the house. I would always lie and say my aunt was out shopping, or getting her hair cut. I felt ashamed of Penny.

Because I was always off visiting friends, or at school, I didn't see the real Penny. It all came down to the calendar—the large grid of days adorned with symbols and markings. It took a half day of school to discover what these meant. When I walked in the door, I saw Penny sitting on the kitchen floor with a bowl in between her legs. A jug of milk seated next to her. In the bowl was a soggy mash of bread. Penny took a soggy piece and tore it into smaller pieces. She leaned over the bowl, then flicked the bread over her head and shoulders, mumbling and chanting something softly. Penny lifted the milk, poured some over her neck, and let the milk run down her neck onto the bread and onto the floor. Then she poured more of the milk over the bowl of bread and increased her voice. She didn't stop when she heard me either: Penny just kept going. I walked back outside and sat on the sidewalk.

This was the last day of summer—September 20th. That night Penny told me that every day on the calendar is special. Each day, she said, has its own purpose. This is why she had so many notes on the calendar. She was marking something. She was reminding herself.

Penny said there were days for blood and roses. There were days for stones. There were days for dancing. There were days for immersing herself in water. There were days for conversation. There were days for walking on hands and knees. There were even days for milk and bread. I saw the last one with my own eyes.

What my aunt never explained was why—even though I asked. She either couldn't or wouldn't explain how her rituals connected with anything else in the world. Penny sighed when I asked "Why?" It just *was* that way.

The next morning I found out how deeply ingrained my aunt's rituals were. That was the first time she told me "We're moving." I didn't understand how or why, though I asked. Penny just explained that for each season she had a different house. She said that she would meet me at my school and take me home. It was time to move to the autumn house.

That day at school all I could think about was the future—would I have to go to school elsewhere? Would the fall house be far away? What would it be like? Where would I sleep in the autumn house?

My aunt Penny was there waiting outside of my classroom, as she said she would be. It was surprising: when I saw my pale, gaunt aunt in my school I came to several realizations at the same time. I realized she did care for me, at least enough to track me down. I also realized I had, to that point, never seen my aunt outside of the red summer house. But there she was, in her cardigan, standing against the wall as if she thought she had done something wrong. Maybe she had and I simply wasn't aware of it.

We didn't drive to the fall house—Penny didn't drive. The only possessions Penny brought from the summer house to the fall house were her clothes and the picture of her husband. We walked four blocks and on the other side of Mayhaven Elementary there was an identical street, with an identical house. It was just as tiny as the summer house, with the same narrow living room, the same tiny kitchen, the same attic. The fall house was even furnished with the same exact furniture. The only difference was that the fall house was painted yellow, not red. Everything that could be yellow was yellow.

That fall I got to know the real Aunt Penny, or at least as much as she'd let me. I learned Penny had lucky numbers—3, 7, 15, and of course 27. She also had unlucky numbers—all evens, for starters. Penny told me the reason she never left the house: toxins. She believed the entire world was corrupted by them, by invisible particles. "Truth: they exist," she said. Until she told me, I didn't know Aunt Penny cleaned every night after I went to sleep. I didn't know the name of the woman who bought food for Penny was named Linda. I had never seen Linda, but Penny assured me she existed.

"I don't have very many friends," Penny said. She said this sitting in her identical armchair, in her identical (but yellow) room. She crossed her legs when she said it, and I took this to be of vast significance. I just didn't know what it meant. Then she said no more on the subject. Since Penny didn't believe in games, I did my housework. Penny said competition was what was destroying humanity.

"Live with both feet flat on the ground," she said once. "Don't get too far away from your own limitations. You have to know what you can do, what you can't."

I nodded.

"But at the same time, wear a mask. Don't be afraid to pretend you're somebody else. This is a way to get along in the world. My hair is not really brown, for instance. I dye it brown."

She was worth listening to. When Penny talked, it was important. I noticed the bible sitting on the counter once. I asked her once if she went to church, if she read the bible.

"No," she said, and pointed once to her head. "It's all up here." Penny told me that the most important thing in life is how to outsmart others, how to use wits. She also said I should adjust my attitude to the situation. These were coping mechanisms, though she didn't call them that.

I started doing well in school. I began to pay attention. I became serious.

Mickey Orlean

The most exciting thing that happened to me when I lived with Aunt Penny had nothing to do with her—it had to do with my cousin Mickey Orlean, the one who later inherited my grandmothers' house. He was the oldest grandkid of the bunch, the son of Aunt Chelsea—who I hadn't yet met at that point in my life. I didn't know then about Chelsea and Penny and all that passed between them.

In the spring my cousin Mickey called Penny. Penny's spring house was entirely orange, an adjustment after the pink winter house. When the phone rang, I was sitting at the kitchen counter with a stool, as always, doing homework. When the phone rang I almost fell to the floor from shock. Nobody ever called Aunt Penny—her numbers were unlisted and since she moved each season most people couldn't keep up with her anyway. Penny answered the phone and told me to go upstairs. Later that night Penny said my cousin would be coming to stay for a while. She didn't tell me much more than that. I would have to discover the rest for myself.

Mickey didn't knock on the door, he just opened it. The first thing I noticed about Mickey was his red handlebar mustache which curlicued into two shell-like spirals on his cheeks. Some-how the effect made me think of two swirly lollipops. Right away, Mickey seemed clown-like, goofy, unfit for the daily seri-ousness that Aunt Penny cultivated on a minute-by-minute ba-sis. In one hand Mickey carried a gigantic purple valise, fringed with frills and tassels. The valise was almost bigger than he was. In the other hand, Mickey balanced a pickle jar. Sloshing inside the pickle jar were three black fish. Their eyes bobbed above the water line, and they looked lethargic, on the edge of death. Mickey wore a thick, hooded coat, and a green and white polka-dotted scarf. He was sweating.

Aunt Penny sat in her regular chair and Mickey sat in the other one. This left the floor for me. Mickey unwrapped his scarf and unbuttoned his coat, and wiped his brow with the back of his hand. Aside from his odd, garish dress, Mickey's face seemed tattered, torn apart by something. His chin sagged. His eyes seemed watery and secluded, his mouth permanently affixed in a slight downturn—as if he were constantly on the edge of weeping.

"Whew," he said, exhaling dramatically. "It's good to finally *be* here."

After Mickey introduced himself, he withdrew a canister of fish food from his pocket and tapped the flakes from it into the pickle jar. Then he told us he was traveling for two months straight, driving around the country. Mickey said he'd always wanted to see the world, and now he was.

"I'm glad as hell to see you, Aunt Penny," he said. Then he reached into his coat pocket again, this time withdrawing a corncob pipe. I didn't know what it was at the time, but I learned soon enough. He snapped a lighter and puffed on the pipe. I watched Aunt Penny. I expected her to put the kibosh on Mickey's smoking, but she didn't. People surprise. I told myself maybe it had something to do with her numbers, with some grand scheme that I couldn't even visualize. More likely, she was just trying to be accommodating. An appearance by Mickey was rare. More to the point, an appearance by any relative was rare. Aunt Penny was a hermit by choice, but sometimes I wondered about that.

Aunt Penny crossed her hands on her lap, and she nodded at Mickey. Mickey twirled his handlebar mustache in his fingers. I watched the mustache hair unfurl and then snap back into place, seemingly even more curly and bouncy than before. He puffed on his pipe and his feet bopped with nervousness. I expected him to cry, but he didn't. Instead, Mickey wiped his mouth with his hand, once, twice, three times. When he lifted his hand, Mickey's mouth swooped up into a smile. Mickey was the first real salesman I had ever met. And he could talk with the best of them. He could talk until you never wanted to hear another person talk again.

"Let me tell you the saddest story you will ever want to hear," he said. "It's sad, but it's not too sad. It's sad in a way that will make you happy, if this makes sense. This makes sense to me. I mean, sometimes if you hear a sad song, the natural instinct is to feel better. This is always how I feel at least. I mean, I'm not sure if this is how you feel, but it's how I feel. So anyway, I was down along the border. Desert. Scrubby plants. Mexico a mile or two away. Hot. Dry. I was down there when I came across a series of hills. They call them buttes. But they're hills. Flat hills. They're like mountains if you cut the peak off with a pair of gigantic scissors. These buttes are like that. And anyway, I decided just for kicks to hike to the top of one of these buttes. I decided it might be nice to get a clean view of the area, to see what it's like. I wanted to have a three-hundred-and-sixty-degree view of Mexico and the desert and everything around it."

"So I hiked up this butte, and when I got to the top I couldn't believe what I saw. At the top of this butte, at the top of this mountain with the top cut off, were thousands and thousands of Monarch butterflies. You know, the black and gold ones. They're beautiful. They're huge, with wings a foot long. And every single butterfly was dead, or at least dying. I mean, a few flapped a wing. Either that or it was the wind catching the wing. Have you ever heard anything so sad in your entire life? Thousands and thousands of dead beautiful butterflies. I had to sleep up there on the butte that night. How could I not? I wanted to pay my respects to the dead butterflies. Next day, I bought the fish. Something to replace them. I needed something alive."

Mickey puffed on his pipe, and he lifted up the jar of fish with both hands, and I watched the water slosh in the pickle jar and onto the floor, and onto Mickey's arm. The fish circled slowly in the jostling water. Mickey would talk like this and the only thing Aunt Penny and I could do was listen. So we did.

Mickey stayed with Aunt Penny for nearly a week, though because he talked so much it felt as if it were much longer. He called it a "vacation from his vacation." Aunt Penny never complained, but I know Mickey interrupted her routine. With Mickey there, she couldn't sit in silence. She couldn't communicate with her husband, or disappear on intergalactic travels. At least once Mickey woke up—which wasn't until nearly noon each day.

When I returned home from school, Mickey would be up and running. I'd rarely see him eating or drinking (he was "anti-ingestion," or so he said). But he'd almost always talk my ear off, tooling with his handlebar mustache and telling some story or another. Mickey seemed unwilling to keep the fish out of sight, and he insisted on clutching the pickle jar between his knees. Even though it was April and becoming warm, Mickey always wore his scarf. And of course all the stories he told related to his travels, as if he were sharing an oral equivalent of a slide show.

"There was this one woman I met down south," he said. "She was a wild one. She was tall and thin as a sapling. Her neck was the size of my arm, and her head was just as long. At any rate, when I met her the first words out of her mouth were, 'I'm somebody special.' That's what she said. I'm not usually impressed, so I thought I'd ask her how she was special. I wanted to know what she meant by 'special.' So I asked her and she told me, and what she told me was, 'I'm the daughter of someone very famous.' She wore this purple dress that hugged her curves. The dress was affixed with some kind of gold trim. It looked like it was made out of real gold. And she wore enough jewelry to break a horse's neck."

I had so many questions, but my questions were mostly about Mickey himself. He wasn't like anybody I had met up to that point. I wanted to know *his* story. He puffed on his corncob pipe, tapped the smoked residue into his hand, and then balled that into his pocket.

"She was the daughter of a very famous basketball player, or at least she claimed she was. She said she was going to write a book, that she was going to tell the world who she was. She had a face that looked like a combination of a turtle and a snake, if that makes any sense. At any rate, we became friends, if you know what I mean. She said maybe I could help her. Well, who knows what her real story was. You can't trust a woman who wears a purple dress, can you?" He winked at Aunt Penny, but Aunt Penny didn't say a thing. She looked worn to a nub, and it was only three o'clock.

"And I met this man down there, just a few towns away. For a living he spent time in traffic. Isn't that a way to earn a buck? Anyway, I went with him once. He would sit in traffic and take notes. I wasn't sure how those notes translated into money, but it did for him. Everyone hates traffic. Traffic wears you down. It breaks your spirit. Well, this guy loved traffic. 'What I like,' he said, 'is watching people suffer. People don't have to suffer enough anymore. These days everything is easy. Traffic upends all that,' he said. The guy had a point. Oh, and he let me crash at his house for a couple days. Beautiful house in the suburbs, and this guy never painted. Never cut his lawn. Never took care of anything. He said it just didn't matter. His neighbors seemed to disagree. Boy, did they ever."

And Mickey could go on and on like this for hours and hours upon end. He would stop only if both Aunt Penny and I stood up and left the room entirely. Even then, he'd talk for a few more minutes thinking we might be within earshot. So this is what we began doing. Penny would mumble something about having to fix dinner or what-have-you; I would follow her.

Otherwise, Mickey would just keep going. He didn't ask me a single question. He was a talker, not a listener. He only asked Penny a question if he needed something. When we would eat, he would keep talking. He would tell stories as if that were just his way of breathing. I began to miss the contained silence Aunt Penny cultivated.

Mickey: "Then there was this woman who was so beautiful, no man would marry her. And she was. I mean, this woman was tall, with the most pristine perfect face and a body to match. I met her at a bus station. My car was on the fritz at this point, so I thought, what the heck, I'll take a bus up the coast for a while, then head back. I decided to fix my car later, when I was in the mood. This whole trip is about self-exploration anyway," he said. "That's what traveling is all about. I mean people travel so that they can take what is outside their window and make it theirs. And that's what I'm doing."

He twiddled with his handlebar mustache, swallowed, caught his breath and then continued. We sat on the stools in the kitchen. Mickey stood hunched beneath the ceiling.

"So this beautiful woman, not only was she beautiful, she was also intimidating. She was brilliant. She had memorized books upon books and could quote them. She could out-argue me. She knew every capital of every country. She would smoke cloves and use the word 'lover.' 'Oh lover,' she would call to me. 'Could you come and give me another of those neck massages? Come on over here, lover.'"

And then something surprising happened. This was after three or four days of listening to Mickey. Penny was in the middle of taking a drink of water, and even through the glass

I could see her eyes constrict. Then, gracefully, she placed her glass on the counter. Mickey was still going on and on about this woman. I didn't understand half of what he said: I was just a first grader. I thought he was funny and odd, but other than that I still didn't know what to make of him.

"That's enough," Penny suddenly said. "No more."

Mickey's face froze, then crumpled, as if Penny had just shot him in the heart. With both hands he smoothed his handlebar mustache down, and he stopped speaking mid-sentence. Then, for a moment, nobody said anything, nobody moved.

"Oh," Mickey said. He looked at me, then he looked at Penny. His face continued to deflate. "Okay." Then he stumbled into the living room with his fish. I thought for a moment he would walk right out the front door, but instead I could hear him slump onto the floor. I could hear the water from his pickle jar sloshing between his legs.

"I guess you don't want to hear the story about the optimist," he said. "That's a pick-me-up."

This was the last we heard of Mickey that day.

The next morning Mickey was awake before I was. Aunt Penny was sitting in silence in her chair, the curtains drawn closed as always. I sat at the counter eating my cereal before I had to go to school. Mickey cleared his throat and sat on the other bench.

"Well, cousin," he said. "I'm hitting the road today. Back to walking the earth."

I spooned my cereal into my mouth.

"About that optimist though," he said, whispering. "This guy who traveled with me for some time. Quite a lot of time actually. He lost his wife. She died in a freak camping accident. Tree fell on her. Anyway, he also lost his job, and two weeks after his wife died he was dismembered in the sawmill where he worked. That was before he got fired. This guy was the happiest man you could ever meet. Big smile on his face. Always joking around. 'Luck evens out,' he said. 'Everything is going to work itself out in the long run.' How could I not believe this guy? He had a perfect life and it was ruined. There he was though. That's faith. *That* is faith."

Like I said, Mickey was a salesman. I realized much later that what he was selling was himself. At the time, I was sad to see him go. Even though I was glad when quiet returned to the house, I missed the stories. I was young and alone. Any distraction from routine was a perk. A week after he left, Mickey sent a postcard thanking Aunt Penny for her generous hospitality and wishing us both well. On the front of the card was a field of orange and pink flowers. A stream trickled in the background and I wondered if Mickey sat by that stream, telling his stories to someone who would listen, a stranger.

I knew how he felt.

True Love

It was an adjustment when Uncle Davis returned for two weeks that winter. At first it seemed as if Uncle Davis was just a male version of Aunt Penny. Aunt Penny sat in the dark in her chair. Once Davis arrived, he sat across from her. In the dark. In a chair. The only difference was this: together they smiled—broadly, without shame. Usually Aunt Penny's face was fixed into a stony mask. Aunt Penny had rituals that she liked to practice according to the day of the week, the month of the year. Davis did too. Penny liked to clean at night. Davis did too. I thought initially that these were things that Penny did to make up for her husband's absence. What I saw was the opposite: Penny's rituals had to do with not forgetting what they did together. My aunt loved to be in the presence of her husband.

This left little room for a castaway nephew. I began to feel unwanted. I would stare at the pink walls and the pink upholstery and the pink candlesticks. I felt like the world was against me.

Uncle Davis didn't seem to acknowledge me. A bespectacled, slightly taller version of Penny, he too wore a cardigan, and kept his hand quietly pressed to his thighs. He had dark hair and at first he wore a white naval uniform with a hat. In many ways, Davis and Penny seemed to be more brother and sister than husband and wife. I didn't think of this then; now I do. Penny didn't tell me that their two weeks together was their "honeymoon time." She didn't tell me that, since this was the only time they saw each other throughout the year, it was quite sacred. I learned the hard way.

The first few days Davis was there, I was still in school. This actually made it easier. By the time I came home from school, I could do my homework, or I could play marbles with my friends. But by the time the winter holiday was in order, I didn't have anything to do other than to play marbles with my friends. I could only play for about half an hour before I became bored. I became bored of marbles a lot during Davis's stay. If I never see a marble again in my life I'm fine with that.

Once I ran out of things to do with my friends, I began walking around outside. The city wasn't cold enough in the winter to make life miserable, but it was cold enough. And it was rainy. This rain was worse than snow, and it seemed as if I walked around the city in a constant wet drizzle. I was only seven, but because my grandmother taught me homing instincts at an early age I felt as if I could never get lost. And I didn't. I could always remember how to get back to Penny's house.

The problem was that I didn't always know *when* to go back to Penny's house. During the day they seemed to spend less and less time sitting in the dark in the living room, and more time in Penny's room together. I didn't know then what they might be doing. I just felt left out. The moaning and the panting made me worry. I thought someone was sick or hurt, but I didn't dare disturb them. Part of me was green with envy then. I wanted to spend time with Penny; I had grown accustomed to her. I even wanted to spend time with Davis. Instead, the door was shut, locked, and I was left to make do on my own. These were times when I brought out the picture of my parents. I would look at it and wonder where in the world they were. I would wonder if I would ever have the chance to be ordinary. A regular kid.

I discovered the city when I was outside by myself: my friends could only spend so much time with me. Once Christmas approached, they were with their parents, their families. For Christmas, Penny gave me a "thought-present." She created a shape in her mind, she said. Then she gave that to me in a "thought exchange." She asked me to do the same, and I did. Or I think I did. I don't want to say what I created. It was half animal, half plant. It was every color and it protruded in every odd angle. It didn't make much sense. Penny and Davis were together, in the room. When I was there they seemed interested only in each other. When I wasn't they didn't seem to notice. So I wandered.

I walked from the leafy streets to the shops where an old man swept the sidewalks with a push broom and where fat women with maroon moles on their cheeks sold dingy orange flowers in the middle of the street. The stores were empty. Above the stores, where people lived, I could see the bright Christmas lights and I could hear the sounds of children laughing. I didn't mind, or this is what I told myself. It was cold and a fine drizzle leaked from the gray clouds.

I walked to the warehouses and factories along the river. I didn't know what they were called then: the buildings just looked huge. The brick facades cast deep shadows over the water and the water slapped against the pilings. Steam dribbled from the smoke stacks. I didn't see anyone there. I saw an abandoned bicycle chained to a sign in the median strip. I watched cars stream from the highway onto the road by the warehouses, and the fire hydrants and newspaper boxes squat by the side of the road. I listened to the signs shimmy in the wind. Cans and bottles bobbed in the water. So did a deflated basketball. Penny said things have souls. I didn't know what she meant until I walked through the city.

By the bus station a blind man played the trumpet for change. It was Christmas, so the bus station was empty. The wall of the bus station was plastered with brassy posters. The bright colors made me blink. I thought of Penny's pink winter house. I wondered if Penny had ever been on a bus. "Hey you," the blind man called out, but I didn't say a word.

That day I felt as if I understood loneliness. I had known about loneliness before, from living with my grandmother, from living with Aunt Tess, and then Aunt Penny. I just didn't know the word. But this was the first time I really *felt* loneliness. I thought of the woman I met on the bus on the way to stay with Aunt Tess. She knew what I felt.

I walked further away from Aunt Penny's house, toward the bridge. I passed the taxi station, where several men huddled under an overhang. Other men talked outside, smoking cigarettes. They watched me and didn't say a word. I passed alleys rimmed with stagnant puddles. I passed clusters of signs and two women arguing in the street with their paper bags stuffed with food. I didn't see movie theaters or hear music. I saw churches far behind me, and those were stained with pollution. I didn't hear laughter. The train tracks hummed, though I didn't hear a train. Pigeons squawked over scraps. A cemetery slumped on a hill overlooking the tracks.

I was almost to the bridge when the policeman pulled up next to me in his car. He had all kinds of questions. His face was wrinkled with worry, and he held his knees as he talked to me. His hair was peppered with gray. He asked me how old I was. He asked me why I was alone. He asked me if I was okay. He asked me where I lived. Then he drove me to Aunt Penny's. From the window of the car I could see the dogs chained to fences. I could see the men pushing grocery carts.

I knew I would, at least in some ways, always wander.

Aunt Penny and Uncle Davis apologized to the policeman, and they apologized to me. They must have felt guilty or shamed afterwards because from that point on, Uncle Davis treated me like his own son. When I told him that I loved chess, he played with me. When I told him I liked the country, he drove me out into the farmland for the day. When I told him I liked the woods he drove me out into the woods to walk through them. Then he stopped listening to what I liked. I knew that he wanted to get back to his wife, to spend time with her before he was shipped back out.

At first I thought Uncle Davis didn't have much of a personality. At first I thought that he didn't have as many interesting things to say as Aunt Penny. I thought he was the least complex relative I had met so far. But when he told me he had been in two wars, I started watching him. His brown hair was cut close to his skull. It was oily-looking, as if he sprayed it with Crisco.

Davis told me that he had shot a gun. He told me that he knew how to fly an airplane, a fast one. When I asked him about where he slept, he told me he slept on the aircraft carrier.

"I've killed people," he said. He didn't exactly flinch when he said it, but it was something close. Then he blinked, and his fingers constricted. We were in the car and the shadows from the trees rattled across the road. We were heading home. Davis was driving fast. I don't know if I expected him to ask me why I walked out into the city on Christmas, but I could tell he knew why. Davis was quiet, but he was not a stupid man at all.

"What did it feel like?" I asked him. He clicked his tongue in his mouth and adjusted the heat. I could tell he didn't know what to say, how to answer that. He was probably wondering why I was such a pain in the butt, why I was so nosy, why I was even there interrupting his domestic quality time. He was probably thinking, *I don't even know this kid and he's asking me how it felt to kill a man.*

"It's something you don't want to experience," he said. "You don't feel good about it, that's for sure."

I wasn't sure if I should believe him or not. He didn't seem like a cruel man, but he also didn't seem to want to elaborate.

I wondered how they met. I wondered how they fell in love. In retrospect I think Penny fell in love with his willingness to sit in silence with her. She perhaps even fell in love with the time she was able to spend alone, without him. Maybe they talked in private, but then again Penny claimed they talked in their minds. I suppose they didn't need to use their voices.

When we reached home, the pink enveloped us. For a moment I felt as if we were wrapped in a chocolate box. Penny and Davis didn't embrace, and they didn't kiss. They sat in their chairs and looked into each other's eyes. It was almost eerie to watch. There was nothing I could do.

I walked upstairs and I paused at the door to their bedroom. Penny and Davis sat still downstairs, so I entered their bedroom. I stood at the foot of their bed and smelled the air. It smelled odd, I thought. Different than anything else I had smelled up to that point. The bed was made and it looked neat as always. But the smell was definitely different—sour, pungent. I looked at the picture of Davis hanging on the wall. I looked into the puffy clouds in the background. I looked closer into Davis's tennis-ball-sized eyes: in his pupils I could actually see the reflection of the camera and Penny behind the camera taking the picture. In the lens of her camera I could see a tiny reflection of Davis smiling. I had never noticed this before. All those empty months of the year Penny looked at a picture of her husband, there was a tiny image of herself inside him.

In retrospect, the relationship between Penny and Davis provided me the first template for my own image of love. Penny and Davis were distant; they seemed to be only complete together. Yet at the same time, I realized later how painful this must have been for them. Penny never complained about Davis's absence, but after he left I could see how relentless this was. Still, when they were together they blanked everything else out. They were one, or as close to one as I could understand. For Aunt Penny and Uncle Davis it was all or nothing. I'm sure

I broke several hearts as a result of my own concept of love and what it entailed. This was a concept I inherited.

When Davis left after New Year's Eve my routine with Penny picked up where it left off. I went back to school. Penny retreated back into her world of silence and numbers and secret rituals.

One night I asked Penny about my mother. Suddenly, I just felt the urge.

Penny cleaned her fork with her napkin and continued chewing 27 times, as usual. When she finished she took a long drink from her water and placed the glass directly where it sat before, rotating the glass to its exact previous position.

"Your mother was so much younger than I was," she said. "Thirteen years younger." She told me that when she was sixteen, my mother was only three. Penny told me that when she was eighteen, my mother was only five.

I nodded and held my chin in my hands. I could feel the weight of my own head in my hands. It felt funny to hold it like that, but I wanted to understand how it felt to present myself like an adult would.

Then, for the first time, Penny seemed to show sympathy. Her face lightened, and the brow that she usually kept fixed in a furrow yielded.

"This is only my view," Penny said. "But your mother always seemed wild and wooly. Even when she was young, she would run away from home. Example: once, a neighbor caught her dancing in the middle of a busy street. Expression. Individuality. Romance. Vivacity. Your mother wanted all these things." At the time, I didn't know what these words meant, but I could tell by the way Penny said them that she didn't approve.

My aunt sighed deeply and said that once she moved away from home, she didn't see much of my mother. She said the rest of what she knew about my mother was common knowledge, but it was also based on hearsay. I asked what that meant, and Penny said it meant rumors, talk. Penny said she didn't believe in spreading gossip, or relying upon what other people said. "Why? It takes something *away* from me." She shook her head and said that was all she wanted to tell me about my mother.

"Don't ask me again," she said. "I have nothing more to say. If you want to know more about your mother, ask my sisters."

When the summer cycled back around again, I knew I would be moving on. I could feel my time with Penny was coming to a close. At first this was just a feeling, but the feeling became a greater intuition when I watched Penny's eyes. Instead of glazing past me, they examined. Instead of retreating into a world of silence and astral travel and ESP, Penny's eyes blinked and inspected. I felt like a distraction, a specimen in a Petri dish.

When Penny did speak, it was in the form of a question: "I wonder, should I call your grandmother? Chelsea and I haven't spoken for years, have we? Do you think I should apologize to Aunt Tess?" These started as purely rhetorical questions, but still. As far as I could tell, Penny was thinking about her family for the first time during my stay. I had never heard her even mention her relatives before. As far as I could tell, she thought of herself as an orphan—like me. But she didn't.

At night, I slept in the sweltering attic with the fan blowing hot air on my sweating body. One sticky night I could hear

Penny talking on the phone: this was a novelty. I couldn't hear the actual words, but I knew there were words. Not that I didn't like Penny, but I did feel claustrophobic. And at the same time I missed living with my grandmother. I also missed living with Aunt Tess. I missed looking out the window and seeing trees and fields. I missed the echo of my own voice over the mountainside. I liked the friendships I had developed living with Penny, and part of me wanted to stay with her. Despite the gruffness of my grandmother and the flakiness of Tess, with them somehow I never felt lonely. With Penny I did. I felt like a distant moon circling a remote and icy planet.

I couldn't speak to Tess because their financial situation had gone from bad to worse—they had to put a halt to their phone service. When I had the chance to speak to my grandmother, she cleared her throat and I could hear a loud clumping sound on the other end of the line. I imagined her chopping potatoes or onions the size of footballs.

"Are you being a good boy, Thomas?"

I told her I was. I told her I liked living in the city, that it was different. I knew Gaga hated a whiner. When Gaga spoke to me Penny left the room. This was one of the nicest things she could have done—she gave me privacy. If anything, Penny knew the importance of seclusion. But at this moment, I felt I had nothing left to learn from Aunt Penny. This wasn't true, but at the moment it felt that way.

"Are you listening to your aunt?"

"Yes ma'am," I said. "I help her out around the house." This last part was false, of course. Penny didn't ask for my help. She didn't want my help—it would destroy her methods, her system.

The phone call went like this—more an interrogation than a true conversation. But this was Gaga's personality. She was just being true to form. After she had grilled me, my grandmother let me be. She said she was going to go and chop the wood. She said the only person who had helped her since she put me on the bus was my cousin Mickey, who came to stay with her for about a week.

"That boy never stops talking," she said. "But he's the oldest grandson. So I suppose he has privileges. My daughters should take a page from his book."

I didn't know what that meant at the time, and in retrospect I think my grandmother just liked boys better than girls. I'm sure she always wanted a son. I'm also sure she blamed her husband for not giving her one. So later my grandmother attempted to rectify the matter by giving Mickey her house. He was a man, after all. My grandmother, despite her eccentricities, could defer.

Then my grandmother told me to watch out for Aunt Chelsea. She said that if I thought Aunt Tess was something, I hadn't seen anything yet. I took this to mean that was where I was headed. This was the first I heard of it, and when I was off the phone the only elaboration Penny offered was that she was going to send me on the train.

"The train will take you directly to Chelsea's house," she said. "This will happen on Saturday morning." When Penny said this it was Wednesday. In two days I said goodbye to my friends and packed all my belongings. By this point I was ready to leave Penny and her revolving houses and head games. And then, on a cold Saturday, Penny walked me to the train station and bought me a ticket. I remember it was blustery that day. Papers and leaves blew down the street and around us. Somehow this seemed fitting.

Because I had been on a long bus ride before, I wasn't nervous. But when I sat down inside the train, I didn't see Penny on the platform. I saw the light wash through the high transom inside the station. I watched the pigeons congregate on the top of the station roof. I watched a torn paper bag tumble down the platform and stick to a man's leg. Then the train pulled out of the station, and the city unspooled behind me.

The Breeze

Because I didn't know my parents, I have never known the exact date of my birthday. My grandmother celebrated my birthday on July 22, but this was just a stab in the dark. She didn't know when my exact birthday was either. When I lived with Aunt Tess, we celebrated my birthday on July 25, and when I lived with Aunt Penny we didn't celebrate it at all. She believed in the arcane power of numbers, and said she couldn't celebrate my birthday if she didn't know on exactly which day I was born. "It makes a world of difference," she said. "The constellations shift." At any rate, I knew my birthday was sometime in July, maybe August.

July 27th was the day when I took the train from the city to Aunt Chelsea's—Aunt Penny said that was an excellent day to travel. As I sat all alone on the train, I wondered if I was really eight yet, or if I just thought I was.

By the time I left Aunt Chelsea's house—if you can call where she lived a "house"—I was ten. The two years I spent living with Aunt Chelsea were two of the most difficult, most intense years of my life. Looking back, if I knew what living with Chelsea would be like, I would have never left Penny's re-volving seasonal homes and peculiar introspection. Penny was odd and closed-off, but at least she was stable. I didn't have much in the way of perspective at the time, of course. I was just a child. I would soon find out quite a bit about my family. I would find out that Chelsea was the middle sibling. I would also find out that Chelsea considered herself to be the black sheep of the bunch.

The train trip itself could have given me a clue as to how difficult my stay with Chelsea would be. But at the time I didn't think of it in this way. I just enjoyed watching the land pass by. Or I did until I became too exhausted to notice much of anything. Aunt Penny didn't tell me the train trip would take a day and a half—this is what the one-armed conductor finally told me. The conductor's name was Lynn, though at the time I thought that was only a girl's name.

The landscape offered me enough distraction. The train didn't go through the same kind of farmland as Aunt Tess's. But we did pass farms for hours: yellow and greens with streams running in culverts. I watched the farmland become browner and drier. Instead of chicken coops and pig farms, I saw cows and bulls, and then circular fields of wheat and barley. And then dry sedge. Then dirt and sand. I watched the shadows of buzzards glide over the flatness.

When I woke up, it was dark. When the darkness gave way to light, I saw the desiccated and stony land. I saw miles of pebbled sand and thorny brush, the stone veined with crags and cracks. The sky looked bluer than I had ever seen, and it bled clear to the horizon where it lightened and faded into the brush.

I thought we were close to Chelsea's house, but we were far from it still.

The train continued through this land until the land rose into stones and cliffs and buttes topped with gnarled pines. I looked at the picture of Chelsea that Aunt Penny had given me. In the photo, Chelsea's red hair was pulled back in a ponytail and she looked away from the camera at almost a forty-five degree angle. This gave Chelsea's picture the look of a criminal profile. Her nose looked like a sliding board. Her eyes squinted into the distance, as if searching for a lost friend. Chelsea's face was thin, and her skin was smooth and rich. She was also beautiful—I remember thinking that.

What I didn't see outside the window was as memorable to me as what I did see: houses, buildings, farms, churches, trees. Where were the people?

We pulled into the train station early in the afternoon. I could see the heat simmering from the platform. When I walked out onto the platform, only a few others walked with me from the train. I didn't see anyone waiting on the heat-baked platform. There was no shade and I was tired. A series of flat concrete benches sat against the far wall inside the small, hot station. I sat down on one of the benches and I waited for my aunt. The bench was chipped and decorated with scrawls of red and green graffiti. As I leaned back, I could feel the gum on the belly of the bench. The ceiling fans circled, and I could hear footsteps on the tile floor. I looked up but I could tell it was not my aunt. No red hair. Eventually I fell asleep on the bench.

I dreamed I was in a boat surrounded by people. Ice clinked in glasses and people quietly muttered. A woman in a purple feathered hat stood at the bow of the boat and said she was a princess. She said that we would have to listen to her if we were to make it back to land. The boat bobbed on the waves, and the sun glowered. The air was still. A thick-chested man smirked and pushed the woman from the boat, and the woman sank into the water and then disappeared behind the wake of the boat. Then I noticed that I was rowing. I was the only person rowing the boat. I turned to watch the woman in the water; I kept rowing away from her. Soon the waves consumed the woman. I could see her hat floating on the water. The people in the boat clinked their glasses and talked. A man lifted a piece of shrimp. A fat woman ate cake and slowly licked her fingers. I watched her mouth open and close. Her tongue looked blackened.

I woke up to a hand shaking my arm. I could feel calloused palms and warts. I blinked in the sun and saw Aunt Chelsea. I could tell right away it was her from the sloping nose. The rest of her face looked much different, considerably older than the photo. Her face was deeply scarred, the color of maple syrup. Her red hair was dry and stringy and knotted in places. I could only see the faint shadow of her eyes through her mirrored sunglasses, but they were set deep inside her skull. Her mouth was fringed with small vertical wrinkles that made it seem stitched together. She wore a grimy yellow T-shirt speckled with blood. Her belt was decorated with the tails of animals.

"Let's go, kid," she said. Then she walked away from me. I lifted myself from the bench and saw on the train station clock that three hours had passed. My shirt was sweaty and I felt as grubby as Chelsea looked.

Aunt Chelsea told me to throw my stuff in the bed of her rusted, red pickup truck. Once I saw the pile of dead brown hares, I stopped in my tracks. Their long legs drooped like soggy string all over the bed of Chelsea's pickup.

"Don't you mind them," Chelsea said. "Just throw your shit back there."

The only other adult who ever cussed in my presence was my Uncle Rusty, and he ended up getting stabbed in the leg by Aunt Tess. I didn't like being called "kid" either. And Chelsea didn't apologize once for being so late. I was young but I knew right away that Chelsea would rub me the wrong way. I lifted myself into the bed of the pickup and placed my bags in the bed, as far away from the hares as possible. I just hoped the hares didn't slide down into my bags. This seemed sketchy at best. I looked at the truck, and at my bags in it. I was worried.

"Get in," Chelsea snapped. "I'm tired."

I learned later that when Chelsea said she was tired, what this really meant was that she was tired of *me*. "I'm tired" was usually a warning for something much harsher that she would also say. Chelsea said the air-conditioning was broken. I sat next to a pile of beer cans and old papers. Trash and straws swirled at my feet as Chelsea barreled through the desert.

Aunt Chelsea drove us from the train station down into a canyon, and along a road that paralleled an arroyo. My eyes hurt from the bright glare of the sun. I didn't own a pair of sunglasses, and right away I was afraid to ask Chelsea if she could buy me one. I looked under the crags, into the shadows underneath the rocks. Or I just closed my eyes.

I expected Chelsea to ask me how I was feeling, how my trip went. She didn't. I waited for my aunt to tell me where we were going, what life was going to be like living with her. She didn't say a thing. She pressed her cigarette lighter in and then asked me to hold it so she could light her cigar. She spat the tip of the cigar out the window, and then smoked as she drove. She reached under her seat, opened a beer, and pressed that between her thighs she drove. Aunt Chelsea drove fast. I looked over at the speedometer, and she was going over a hundred miles an hour. I clutched the dashboard.

"I'm eight," I told Chelsea. "I think I turned eight last week." I thought this might catch my aunt's attention.

"I got to get these animals inside," she said. Then she took a massive gulp of beer and licked her teeth. She looked at her mouth in the mirror. "I have to be somewhere later," she said. She didn't seem to be interested in anything other than her dead hares. My aunt didn't nod. She didn't look at me. She just stared straight out at the road and kept driving. Her windshield was splattered with dead butterflies.

We pulled into a gravel driveway and up an incline into the rocks. The shadows in those rocks were deep, and I wondered if caves lay within them. If there were caves, I knew I could take Uncle Rusty's advice and find a place for myself. If not, I knew I would have to find something out there in the desert. Chelsea drove further up the driveway until it stopped at a huge rock outcrop. Tucked under the outcrop was a gray house. Chelsea stopped the truck and shut off the engine. I undid my seatbelt and stepped out into the gravel driveway. I could hear the gravel under our feet. Chelsea opened the bed of the truck and I jumped up into it. Putting two fingers into her mouth, Chelsea let out a violent whistle. I lifted my belongings from the bed of the truck. Blood had run down the bed of the truck and leaked onto my luggage. I suddenly wanted to cry, but I didn't. I carried my stained bags toward the house. I expected my aunt to say something, but she didn't. She stood where she was and didn't move.

An old man stood in front of Chelsea with a large wire basket. He was missing most of his front teeth. Chelsea didn't say anything to him. I turned and watched them. She pointed to the hares, and the old Mexican began lifting the bloody carcasses and placing them into the basket. Chelsea caught up to me and we entered the house. "House" is an overstatement. Chelsea lived in a tin shack under the shade of a rock outcrop.

When I walked inside I could see that it wasn't fancy. The exterior of the "house" was corrugated and corroded. The floor inside was dirt, covered in places by ratty rugs. Spiders and beetles skittered along the walls. The rooms were small and oddly shaped, as if the house conformed to the rock instead of the other way around. Chelsea did have electricity, with a rudimentary kitchen and bathroom. The house smelled of mold and dirt. I could tell I would have to sleep in the living room. From the look of the sheets and the pillows, someone else slept there, too. Chelsea had her own room. The walls of her room were rock.

"There's also a basement here," Chelsea said. "You're not to go into the basement. Understand?" I nodded. I didn't see how she could have a basement in a cave, but it was true. At first I was too tired to care. I drank acerbic tap water, and Chelsea heated me a tortilla and handed me a carrot and a boiled egg. That was it. Then she went back outside to check on the old Mexican. I ate and propped my head beneath a pillow. I lay on the dirt floor until I went to sleep. I could hear voices in the dirt. People walked in and out, but I slept anyway. The old Mexican twitched and thrashed in his sleep. There was nothing else I could do.

It was still dark when Chelsea rattled my arm, waking me up. "Get up," she said. She said it was time for me to earn my worth. I wasn't sure what this meant, but I was about to find out. I didn't know then what time it was (four in the morning), but this would soon be my daily ritual. I would help Chelsea deliver *The Breeze*. The old Mexican man would sleep on the couch until Chelsea roused him. He would drape a towel over his head and hide from the world. I couldn't blame him.

The entire truck was filled with newspapers. Chelsea handed me a mealy apple–I ate half of it and spit the rest into the sand. It was so different than what Gaga fed me. Chelsea was behind the wheel and she drove fast. She showed me what to do the first few times. In a gigantic coffee can, Chelsea kept cracked pink rubber bands. The color reminded me of the walls in my Aunt Penny's winter house. She wrapped several newspapers in rubber bands and slowed down to fifty miles an hour to toss the newspapers into the dark. I couldn't even see a house through the dark, but she did. Chelsea could drive the route in her sleep. I wondered what had happened to the jackrabbits.

"That's all you do," she said. "I'll drive. You band 'em and chuck 'em out the window. I'll tell you when."

That was all there was to it, but the problem was Chelsea drove so fast in the dark, I didn't know when I should throw the newspaper. I could tell if she slowed down to twenty miles an hour, but at fifty it was difficult to know if she was just hugging a curve or if I should throw the newspaper. I couldn't see a thing aside from the triangle of her headlights. The distance between houses was so great it was often difficult to anticipate when the next one was coming around the bend.

"Throw!" she'd bellow. Then she'd slam on her brakes. "What are you waiting for? Throw, dimwit!" I would hesitate to see if I could see *where* I was throwing the newspaper. Aunt Chelsea didn't care, as long as the newspaper landed in the vicinity of the house. "You'd better get it together, kid," she said. "Chuck the thing!"

So this is what I did: I just began to throw the newspaper into the void. I would watch the white tube whirling out of the truck window, and sometimes I could even hear a distant scuffing sound as the newspaper careened across pavement or asphalt or gravel or pebbles. The newspapers landed with a hard scraping sound: no grass, no lawns. I imagined scores of scuffed rolls of newsprint.

The job became easier around 6:00, when the light began to creep into the sky and dribble down onto the road. But by 6:30, we were just about finished. Chelsea drove the entire county, and just about every inhabitant in the area got *The Breeze*. Chelsea said the job helped pay the bills.

"Since you're eating for free, there's a price. The newspapers are the damn price," she said. By the end of the route she was in a better mood. She began smoking her cigar when the light appeared. I asked her why the newspaper was called *The Breeze*.

"Are you kidding me?" I wasn't sure what that meant.

When we returned to her shack I always wanted to fall asleep. But this was when Chelsea put me to work doing other things around the house. She had me dust the antler lamps. She had me dust and shake the many coyote skins. She had me wash the Adirondack chairs. She had me clean the chair made of antelope bones. She had me dust the saws that hung on the wall. Chelsea thought it was especially important for me to sweep. She had me sweep the house for an hour every day, even if there was nothing *to* sweep. "That way, you don't get beetles chewing on you," she said. Chelsea would watch me work. Sometimes she would tell me start all over again. Oddly, Chelsea never had me work with food. Food was not important to Chelsea. Staying with her, I felt lucky to eat at all.

Often she pointed to the red door that led to the basement. "That's the place where you can't go. Understand? I don't want you opening the door. I don't even want you thinking of opening the door." She said that if she found me in the basement it would be the end of my stay with her. Chelsea said she didn't need to watch a kid who couldn't listen to his elders, who didn't show respect. Sometimes I thought Aunt Chelsea didn't trust anyone, not even herself.

On that first full day living with Aunt Chelsea, I asked her where I would be going to school. She said I wouldn't be.

"You're going to be schooled right here. Got all the paperwork myself. *I'm* going to be your teacher." Chelsea cracked another beer open and downed it.

This was the worst news I had heard since I arrived. It was one thing to work and to sleep on the floor—I had done these things before. But I had always *gone* to school. I didn't understand how I could *stay* home and learn anything at all.

"Come 'ere," she said. She pointed to a nicked bureau in her room and said that was where she kept books. She told me to go ahead and open it up, see what I found inside. "Go get yourself a book to read from there. This is the way it's gonna be."

I did as she said. Inside the bureau was a small stack of dusty, yellowed books. Some of the books didn't have covers. Some of the books were missing pages. I picked up one book with a dusty black cover. I didn't know where to start, so I took that one out and closed the rest of them back up in the bureau. Chelsea said I would only need an hour or two every day to do my schoolwork. Her house smelled of dead animals. I wasn't sure if that was from the coyote and fox rugs, the antler lamps, or what. Sometimes the smell seemed to come from the ground itself.

"School's not that important in the scheme of things," she said. "Life is work, doing things."

When I wanted to do school work, Chelsea said she needed me to go out and sweep the driveway. I wasn't sure how to sweep dirt from gravel, but I just went ahead and gave it my best shot. Other times, Chelsea would have me clean the brush. I wasn't sure what to do, and Chelsea didn't give me directions.

Chelsea was as demanding as my grandmother. But unlike Gaga, Chelsea's jobs didn't seem urgent. It seemed as if she just came up with the chores to keep me busy. It seemed as if she just threw in the towel, as if she'd rather just keep me busy until she could figure out what to do with me. When Chelsea was home she was always on the phone, smoking cigarettes and talking to men. I could hear deep voices radiate from the receiver of her phone. The deep timbre sounded menacing to me.

Coyotes and Cutting Boards

One of the only things that made living with Chelsea bearable was Felix, the old Mexican. He was kind to me, and he shed light on the way things really were. He began with the saws I dusted. He saw me standing on a chair in the sour light, dusting the saws with a rag. I could feel Felix watching me, but I didn't care. I liked the company.

After a few minutes he asked me if I knew where the saws came from.

"They were used in the Mexican-American war. They cut legs from the injured soldiers." He had an accent, but I was surprised at how well he spoke English. Later Felix would tell me that he had lived in this country for over forty years, that this country was his in a way that Mexico wasn't. He just thought of himself as an Americano. But Felix also told me he was part Hopi, and that made him different in the first place.

Soon enough I would find out why the newspaper was called *The Breeze*. A few days after I arrived at Aunt Chelsea's, the wind picked up. The sun was setting and I sat on the dirt floor trying to read through the remaining dirty light that trickled through the window. Felix reclined on the sofa with his feet up. This is when the wind began gusting. At first it began as a gentle breeze, and then it picked up, increasing minute by minute. Once the sun began its final descent under the horizon line, the wind was at gale force. Sand and pebbles and sticks and bits of brush pinged against the walls of Chelsea's house. I hadn't a clue where Chelsea was, and I didn't care. Felix closed and latched the makeshift plywood shutters, and told me to hide under the sofa, just in case.

"Sometimes the windows explode," he said. I couldn't believe what I was hearing.

"It happens from time to time. Irregular wind."

The wind was ferocious almost every day, battering the shell of Chelsea's house, clawing at her shack. I don't know how her home held up that night, but I lay on the dirt ground, in complete darkness, terrified that the wind would lift the structure of the house into the next state, and Felix and me with it.

Felix calmed me. He said that Chelsea's house had suffered much worse wind than this. "This is nothing," he said. Chelsea's house appeared to be thrown together, but Felix said what it had going for it was location. Tucked into the rock itself, the structure was fairly protected compared to the homes that lay exposed to the elements out on the flat.

To settle me in the howling wind, Felix told me stories. First he told me his own. As a child, his family was so poor he often ate insects and lizards and snakes to survive. He didn't own a single pair of shoes until he was fifteen. He owned two shirts. When he was sixteen Felix got a job working for a man who caught wild parrots and parakeets and sold them illegally in The United States. Felix was one of the men assigned to catch the parrots. Felix hated his job, but he was doing the best that he could. Felix made a decent living, and was eventually able to buy a small house near a river. He was even well-off enough to attract a woman from a higher class, a woman named Rosa.

Rosa loved Felix for who he was. She loved his sweetness. She loved his gentleness, the way he cared for her. The problem was her family didn't approve of Felix at all. Felix was poor. Rosa and Felix decided to elope, to run away to a town on the far coast of Mexico.

"But her brother, Carlos, found out," Felix said. "Rosa told one of her friends, and this friend told Rosa's brother. On the day when Rosa and I were supposed to run away to get married, Carlos killed Rosa. He shot her in the head and dumped her body in the river. That was when I knew that if I wanted to live, I needed to leave immediately."

So Felix left in the middle of the night, first walking, then hitching rides for days and days. Felix headed north to the American border. He loathed the idea that his few possessions were lost and that all the money he spent upon his small house had gone up in flames. But Felix also knew that he had made it through life with much less, and that he could start over. After years of picking fruit and digging potatoes, Felix met Chelsea and she hired him as her assistant.

"Your aunt rescued me. I felt like a slave before her. I owe her so much," Felix said. "We have a lot in common."

Felix then told me the story of Chelsea. By this point the wind was even stronger, and I clenched my hands around the legs of the sofa, hoping that the walls of the shack didn't bend under the thrust of the wind.

"Chelsea was married once, too," Felix said. "A long time before I came here."

Felix told me that Chelsea was once married to a holy man, a pastor. This I found hard to believe. When Chelsea was young, Felix said, she was very devout—the most religious of all her sisters, the only one who actually wanted to go to church. Chelsea was never good at school, and she never pretended to be. Growing up, Chelsea told my grandmother that instead of school, she wanted to dedicate herself to a higher calling. When Chelsea was eighteen she met Peter. Peter was nearly forty, but Felix said he fell in love with Chelsea as soon as he laid eyes upon her. She was one of the most active members of his congregation, and Peter confided in Chelsea that he was lonely, that he missed the touch of a woman. A year later, Peter and Chelsea were married.

Marriage between Peter and Chelsea was perfect—the best time of Chelsea's life, Felix said. They were truly in love with each other: they hated to be apart for more than even an hour or two. They would pray together. Chelsea would help Peter with church activities. Peter taught Chelsea so much about the Bible and the ways of a faithful life.

Their happiness was short-lived though. One day Peter had to drive far out into the desert to visit a woman, to offer her final rites. The area where Peter drove was one of the most remote in the entire country—water was nowhere to be found. On the drive back to his house, Peter's car conked out, and Peter only had a small amount of water with him. The desert was over a hundred degrees that day. If only another car or truck had driven past, Peter would have lived. But not a single person saw Peter attempting to make it back home on foot. No one saw

Peter collapse by the side of road, there on the asphalt in the middle of the baking desert.

"Some say Peter was eaten by coyotes before he died of thirst. Others say that he died first, and then the coyotes ate him. Either way, by the time Chelsea found her husband's body, it was mostly bone. Chelsea knew coyotes ate carrion. She has always blamed them and the other animals of the desert for taking her happiness from her."

Even with the wind tearing at Chelsea's house, I could tell that Felix loved my aunt Chelsea. If I could go back to that time in my life I would ask Felix why he didn't act upon his own feelings for my aunt, but at the time I was only a kid with a kid's limited understanding. Regardless, though Felix had been in America for many years, I know he wouldn't have felt comfortable approaching a gringa. There was an invisible barrier to him.

Soon enough Chelsea began just disappearing for days, leaving me with Felix. On those days, *The Breeze* simply wouldn't get delivered. Early in the morning, the man from the paper would drive by in his truck, dumping a load of newspapers next to the house. By the next morning, yesterday's papers would still be sitting where the man had dumped them. After three days of this, Chelsea lost her delivery job. The stacks of newspaper stayed where they were, yellowing in the sun. Felix and I would have delivered the newspapers ourselves, but we didn't have a vehicle. When the wind picked up, Felix and I had to pick up all the newspapers strewn all over the driveway. The wind took some of the newspapers and blew them out into the desert. We piled rocks on top of the newspapers we could catch. Chelsea never noticed.

When I would ask Felix where Chelsea was, he would shake his head. I could tell he knew, but he wouldn't say. The most I could get out of him was: "She's out looking for trouble." It was as if Chelsea just gave up.

Things quickly went from bad to worse. Chelsea returned home, looking as if she had died and been brought back to life. Her breath reeked of alcohol and cigarettes and her skin looked leathery. Her clothes were tattered. She didn't say anything. She went directly to bed.

When she awoke that evening, Felix told Chelsea about the newspaper job. Chelsea didn't say a thing. She poured herself a glass of orange juice and downed it. She ate a piece of plain bread. She pointed at me.

"What're you looking at?" I shook my head. I looked away. "You're nothing. You're just a shit," she said. She pointed at me and told me I'm lucky I even have a place to sleep.

Chelsea knew how to scrape by. The next morning she woke me up before the sun rose. She gave me a hardboiled egg and a glass of milk, telling me I had two minutes for breakfast. She threw a beer can at the wall above Felix's head, rousing him. Felix got two eggs and a cup of coffee.

Aunt Chelsea didn't explain where we were going that morning, but Felix didn't look surprised. He told me Chelsea's story made her unpredictable. "Be patient with your aunt," he said. "Please."

Chelsea drove us down the same road where we had delivered *The Breeze*. But this time she kept driving. We didn't see any cars on the road. Then she drove us down into a small canyon. The high cliffs surrounded us. The dry riverbed slashed through the rock, through the land. In an empty area of the desert, Chelsea pulled us off the road, next to a serrated rock formation.

"This is a good place," she said. Felix nodded. Chelsea handed him a box of black plastic bags, and she shut off the engine. She pulled two rifles out of the bed of the truck and handed one to Felix. Felix looked older than before. Chelsea pulled a ratty straw hat over her eyes and draped binoculars around her neck and walked slowly and quietly away from the road. She lifted her head high as she walked, and Felix and I followed her. We walked for an hour and then some.

Eventually Chelsea looked through the binoculars. She pivoted left and right across the dry riverbed, fixing her gaze down the bed. This is when she began humming in a low resonance that reverberated around the canyon. Then she began chanting and humming, humming and chanting. She looked through the binoculars as she hummed. I looked at Felix, but he stared straight ahead where Chelsea looked.

"Don't move," Felix whispered. "It's okay."

Soon I could see movement in the distance—animals. I could see dust. Then I could hear the sounds of running. I wished I could see through the binoculars. I wanted to know what was coming my way. And I was very afraid. Chelsea continued humming and chanting.

My heart hammered in my chest as I watched the coyotes run toward us. There were seven coyotes in all, and I thought for sure they would go for our legs. I thought they were starved. I thought they were angry. I grabbed onto Felix. But the coyotes stopped in front of Chelsea, standing at attention. The coyotes were much larger than I expected, and they looked more like wolves than I thought—gray and brown fur, black tails. Felix would later tell me that the coyotes in this area were larger than most, and more numerous. The coyotes looked at Chelsea and didn't seem to take their eyes from her.

By this point, Chelsea had let her binoculars fall back around her neck. She lifted her rifle and Felix lifted his. One by one, Chelsea and Felix shot the coyotes. Oddly, the coyotes didn't move. It was as if they were drugged, or stunned, or hypnotized. They just stood there, letting themselves get shot. And one by one they fell onto the desert floor. They trembled and convulsed and died. One by one the coyotes stopped moving until the only discernible movement was the wind through their fur.

When the coyotes were dead Felix approached. He pulled a knife from a scabbard attached to his belt buckle and slit the throat of each coyote first, for good measure. He waved me to him. I held the plastic bags open so he could place a coyote in each. The blood ran down his arms, onto his shirt, onto his pants, onto his boots. He wiped his bloody hands on his pants.

On the way back to the truck, Felix carried four bags, Chelsea carried two, and I carried one. Nobody talked for a while. Once we loaded the coyotes into the bed, Chelsea ignited the engine.

"That was good," she said. "That helped."

Eventually I turned to Chelsea, asked her about my mother, about her sister.

"We weren't close," Chelsea said. "I didn't know her all that well. She was just a sister to me. It was a long time ago. What the hell do you want to know?"

I didn't know what else to say.

Felix looked at Chelsea, but he didn't say anything. There was a look of recognition.

I was exhausted, and I slumped against Felix's side for a pillow. The air was hot and still. Chelsea drove fast and I could feel the hot air blow against me. While I was sleeping I dreamed. I dreamed I was walking down a huge marble hallway with large transom windows. The light from outside was red, and it leaked into the hallway. Large blue birds with long blue tails flew past my head, screeching down the hallway. I kept walking through the hallway. When I reached the end of the hallway, there was a door. Above the door was a huge twiggy nest, and in the nest were hundreds of blue birds. The blue birds looked at me, and I looked at them. The door seemed minute compared to the birds. I could see a heavy silver lock on the door. The lock swayed in the wind created by the wings of the birds.

When we returned to Chelsea's house, Chelsea nodded to Felix and Felix went directly to the bed of the truck and withdrew the black plastic bags. Felix asked me to help him, and I did. He whispered that we were going "downstairs." This would be my chance to see the basement. I knew I might never get another one.

Carrying several coyotes on each shoulder, Felix withdrew a small silver key from his pocket and slid it into the lock on the red basement door. He pulled a string and a light came on above us.

"Hello," he said. I thought this was purely rhetorical. I thought Felix was testing the echo of the basement stairwell. A second later I heard a woman's voice reply: "Hello, Felix." We walked down the wooden steps. The walls were made of rock. The air was cool and moist. The staircase was long. Around the looming shape of Felix I could see lights below—green and blue lights reflecting against the rock walls. We walked down into the rock.

Once we reached the bottom of the staircase, we had to walk through a tunnel. The tunnel was long and thin, and Felix had to duck. The green and blue lights became more visible and I could hear music filtering through the tunnel toward us. The music sounded peppy and upbeat and the drums in the music reverberated against the stone walls. We walked through the tunnel. The further we walked through the tunnel, the more Felix had to stoop to avoid hitting his head.

I had never seen men and women like these. They were my size, but the man wore a full beard and the woman looked like a regular woman, only much smaller. The man lifted one leg, as if he were doing calisthenics. The woman had a pleasant, open smile. She held her hand over her heart. They met my eyes and then they glanced at each other. Both the man and the woman were dressed in black, and the man's hands looked scratched and raw. They were extremely pale, almost translucent.

"Welcome, welcome," the woman said. She pointed to the bags of coyotes, and then to the table in the corner of the room. The table was covered with dozens of stuffed animals. Raccoons.

Skunks. Ground squirrels. Birds. Foxes. Coyotes. "You can put those down over there, under the table."

The room was actually much larger than any that Chelsea had upstairs—and nicer. The floor was covered with grey carpeting. Books lined the walls. A small television sat on an oak dresser. A radio sat on the counter. Green and yellow and pink abstract paintings adorned the walls. Two black doors were set in the wall. The room smelled like moldering flesh. This was the scent I'd detected above, in Chelsea's house.

The woman introduced herself as Priscilla, and the man shook my hand. His name was Finnegan. A small boy walked out of the far right door. He was tiny—the size of a cat at most. Finnegan said the boy's name was Remy, four years old.

As Felix told them about our hunting expedition, my mind floated. For the first time in my life, I realized I was surrounded by a normal family. Of my relatives I had lived with up to that point, not one had a normal nuclear family. Aunt Tess's family came closest, but hers was marred by dysfunction and violence. So it was disconcerting for me to see a man and a woman work as a team, in synch.

I expected someone to comment upon how Chelsea was able to lull the coyotes into sacrificing themselves. Felix didn't say a thing about it, and neither did Finnegan or Priscilla. I learned that these were the situations where I had to assert myself, when I had to ask a question. The woman cocked her head at me.

"Would you like some tea?"

"Sure," I said. I stood to the side of Felix, clutching at his thigh. I must have been more nervous than I realized: my hands were trembling. It wasn't just the hunger.

"How about some crackers? We have some delicious gouda." Priscilla's cheeks were ruddy, and her eyes glittered. She had the look of a woman who had survived an ordeal and was grateful simply to be alive. I watched her make the tea and arrange cheese and crackers on a plate. Finnegan walked over to the table and opened one of the black plastic bags. He rolled back the bag and lifted the coyote's head from the bag, glancing at her face, her coat. Felix said that Finnegan did work for Chelsea. He did the skinning, the gutting, the taxidermy work. Finnegan said he had other clients as well, but Chelsea always came first.

"What a beauty," Finnegan said. Felix nodded solemnly.

"I hate doing it," Felix said. "But…"

"Right," Finnegan said. "It's either them or us."

"I suppose," Felix said.

Priscilla invited us to sit down at the table, and Remy danced silently around the room to the music. He circled his tiny arms and lifted his head to the ceiling. Finnegan rolled his head and laughed.

"How is school going for you?" Priscilla asked me. Felix looked at me, and his head seemed to drop. I didn't know what to say. I didn't want to bad-mouth my aunt, but then I didn't want to lie.

"Okay," I said. I slid my hands under my legs and sat on them, as if by doing so I would keep my mouth shut as well. Finnegan watched me. I thought I saw pity in his eyes. He seemed shrewd, street-smart.

"What are you doing?" he asked.

Priscilla poured me a tiny cup of tea, and I ate a cracker with cheese. The cheese was delicious, almost sugary. I thought of the advice my Aunt Tess gave me—to establish myself as a bully so others would fear you. In a school of one, I didn't have a chance.

"I'm reading," I said.

"What are you reading?" Priscilla asked. I felt as if I were under investigation. I didn't know then that questions were also a sign of interest, of caring. I told them, and Priscilla placed her hand back over her heart, as if she were holding it in place. Her eyes washed over her book collection.

I wanted to ask why they lived down in the basement. I wanted to ask them why I had never seen them before. I wanted to ask them how they became involved with my aunt in the first place. Instead, I sat on my hands. And when I wasn't sitting on my hands I drank tea, ate cheese and crackers.

Priscilla told me I was always welcome to come down and read anything in her library. She said they weren't too busy, and that they wanted me to feel as if I could always visit.

I helped Felix bring Finnegan the rest of the coyotes, and then we walked back upstairs to sleep. Chelsea was already gone. Her house sat in the dark, and the wind wailed.

Chelsea began spending more and more of her time away from home. It was as if she just gave up on me. It got so that I would only see her once or twice a week. Felix and I had to fend for ourselves. The refrigerator and cupboards were often empty. So Felix and I began spending our time down with Finnegan and Priscilla and Remy. In addition to the fact that they were kind and supportive, Finnegan owned a scooter. And they in the basement they were completely protected from the terrifying winds.

I began going down to Finnegan and Priscilla each morning. They would feed me ham and bread and fruit and juice and tea. As Finnegan worked on the coyotes, his wife would sit me at the table and teach me math and French. I felt a switch click in my mind again. This was what I needed. Then she had me read stories and poems and history—then we talked about those. When Remy wasn't dancing to the music, even he read. For the first time in months, I felt alive. Finnegan patted my head and told me I deserved better. Priscilla was a sweet lady with a good nature. He asked me about my parents and I told him what I knew. Priscilla said it was a shame that she hoped I could one day live with my parents. It was the first time anyone had said that to me.

I had to force myself to walk back up the stairs to Chelsea's house.

Then Chelsea found out. As Felix told me later, one day she came home and he was sweeping, clearing the brush—doing the work I usually did. I was down with Finnegan and Priscilla, practicing my spelling. From the basement, I could hear Chelsea screaming: "Little shit. That little shit." Then I heard her fling the door open. Her voice pierced the air.

"What did I tell you? What did I tell you about the basement, you little shit?"

I heard her feet pound down the stairs. I wanted to hide. I wanted Finnegan and Priscilla to protect me. I looked around frantically for something with which I could protect myself. I grabbed the closest object with a handle—a small wooden cutting board.

When Chelsea saw me, I could see she was drunk beyond belief. Her face was bright red, and she stunk of cigars and gasoline and booze. She was cussing and telling me she was going to beat the living hell out of me. Her wild red hair was flailing around the room. She made a grab for me, pushing Priscilla out of the way. I ducked under the table. Then I swung. The wooden cutting board felt heavy in my hand, and I knew it would only take one whack with the edge of it to hurt my aunt. I didn't want to do what I did. As I let the cutting board go, I regretted it. As I felt the solid wood hit Chelsea's shin, I regretted it even more. I knew she would fall.

Then she did. Chelsea grabbed for the tiny chair and the table, but she missed, crumpled over, holding her shin, howling in pain. I ran upstairs as fast as I could. Then I ran out of Chelsea's house and down the driveway, into the desert. I spent the night sleeping in the thorns, on the sand and pebbles. Shivering. The wind was ferocious, and I had to cover my eyes with my hands.

This changed everything. Before hitting my aunt with the cutting board, I was a "good boy." Afterwards, I was an outcast, a degenerate, as useful to her as a dead coyote in a black plastic bag.

When Chelsea and Felix found me the next morning, I was so cold I was almost relieved. She lifted my body into the truck and laid me down next to her. By the way she carried me, I thought her anger had subsided. But in retrospect I think she was just trying to be careful with my body so she wasn't blamed for anything. She carried me with a limp. My belongings were in a heap on the floor.

"Sit up," she said. I did. "We're going for a drive."

Then she drove and didn't say a word. She drove in the opposite direction of the canyon where we killed the coyotes. Chelsea sped up faster and faster. It felt like we were going two hundred miles an hour. I peed my pants. I was afraid she was going to push me out of the truck. She still smelled like alcohol. Her mouth was curled into a tiny fist. Her eyes were focused on one thing. Even her ears seemed angry.

The desert all looked the same—mile after mile of brush and sand and scoured rock. But then the road narrowed and I could see buildings, and suddenly Chelsea pulled off the road into a parking lot next to a white building. She stopped the truck.

"Get out of the truck," she said. She grabbed me by the wrist and dragged me into the building. At first I thought the building was a church. It had the high roof and steeple. The door was locked but she had the key. She turned on the lights, and I could see the inside of the building was a bar—tables and chairs, and a long bar with bottles along the wall. Chelsea walked behind the bar and slammed two glasses on the bar.

"Sit," she said. I lifted myself onto one of the stools and watched her.

She poured herself a big glass of yellow-looking alcohol. She drank it in one gulp. She poured me a glass of clear-looking liquid and slid the glass to me—I hoped it was water, and it was.

"I work here now," she said. "That's why I haven't been home."

"Okay," I said.

I thought Chelsea was going to give me a lecture, but she didn't. She wiped down the counter and I sat there watching her. Chelsea was cut-and-dry. She was a tough woman. And she was through with me—I could see that. I didn't know about the prison time then. I didn't know how deep her trouble ran. But I did know that she probably had zero intention of my staying with her in the first place.

"I'm taking you back to the train station," she said.

Then she did.

What Chelsea didn't tell me at the bar was that she wasn't going to give me a penny. She didn't tell me she was going to abandon me. When she pulled back into the train station, it had only been several months since I had arrived. It felt like years.

"Get out," she said.

I did, but she didn't. She stayed behind the wheel.

"What am I supposed to do?"

She peeled off.

I don't know if she didn't hear me or didn't care. Either way it amounts to the same situation. There I was, a young child, alone in a train station. I didn't have a penny on me, and I didn't know how to contact anybody who could help me. I sat down on the step of the train station. I watched the shadows drift that day. And they did drift. My stomach was knotted. I was utterly alone.

Misery

My entire life wasn't spent in isolation, but at the time it felt like it. I didn't know anything different so it didn't bother me. Since I had already lived with my grandmother and three different aunts, I didn't think much of abandonment. In retrospect, I was glad my grandmother left me in the middle of the woods, forced me to find my way back home.

Sitting there at the train station in the middle of the desert was different though. I didn't know *how* to get back home. I didn't know where home was. I didn't even know where I was going, which relative I would stay with next. Initially I wasn't frustrated. I just figured Aunt Chelsea was upset and would come back and pick me up. I waited. This didn't happen. Then I thought maybe Finnegan and Priscilla would find me and pick me up. This didn't happen either. Slowly, my optimism eroded. Then I became frustrated.

In my bags I found the one photograph I had of my parents. I looked into their eyes, and I wondered where they were. I didn't feel like I had to spend the rest of my life with my parents, but I did want to at least know them. I did want to meet them. I did want them to at least have a round with me, like the rest of my relatives had. I sat in the train station looking at that photograph, trying to figure out the puzzle with my young brain. I just didn't understand.

Then I remembered the woman I met on the bus on the way to Aunt Tess's house. I knew I still had the phone number she gave me in case of emergency somewhere. I pulled out all my clothes and finally found the slip of paper she'd given me way back when. It was the only phone number I had. But I didn't have any money. How could I call the woman? I didn't want to resort to begging, and I didn't know how to at any rate. I was an elementary schooler: I had my own ideas. I didn't want to bother the conductors or the ticket salesmen. Most of all I didn't want pity.

In this case, pity was thrust upon me. I sat on the bench for hours, waiting. I watched the woman talk to her caged parrot, pulling her luggage closer. I watched the couple on the bench murmuring to each other, holding hands, blocking out the world. I watched the old man in the black cowboy hat pace back and forth up and down the station. Mostly though, I watched the one-armed man push the broom up and down the floor of the station. He pushed the broom repeatedly, wedging the broom handle under the crook of his stump to make a sudden turn.

Finally, after hours of sweeping, the one-armed man pushed the broom by me. Then he stopped. The man had sad doggy eyes, a face that looked as if someone had pulled a rug out from under him. I wondered if his sadness was a result of the arm, or something else.

"You here all alone?" he asked.

"Uh-huh," I said. I didn't want to tell him how my Aunt Chelsea left me here. I didn't want to get anyone into trouble. He asked if he could sit down. He leaned the broom against the bench. He withdrew a dirty green cloth from his back pocket and began dabbing his forehead. I didn't see any sweat on his face, but he kept dabbing.

"The heat gets to me after a while," he said. He sighed, and continued dabbing his face. "Where are you going?"

"I don't know," I said.

"You don't have a ticket?"

I shook my head.

"Do you have money for a ticket?"

I shook my head.

The one-armed man looked around, as if he would find a ticket on the floor of the station. He lifted himself from the bench and told me he would be back. I had a feeling he was going to seek reinforcements, but when he returned a few minutes later, he carried a handful of change. He said he would help me make some phone calls, call someone who might be able to help me. I thanked the man.

With the money from the one-armed man, I was able to call the woman I met on the bus. The phone number she left was at a hotel in the city of Misery. I didn't know where Misery was. I didn't know if the woman would still be there. As I listened to the phone ring, the man sat on the bench watching me. After several rings, the hotel operator picked up and I read the name from the piece of paper: Marta Keesley.

"Hold on one moment," he said. "I'll transfer you."

She was still there in Misery.

"Hello," the voice said. Her voice sounded gravelly, as if I just woke her up. I wasn't sure what time it was in Misery. I told Marta who I was, how I knew her.

"Oh yeah," she said. "I 'member you. You gave me the delicious apple on the bus. Right. How are you?"

I told her. I didn't use the word "emergency," but I did say I was in trouble, that my aunt left me at the train station, that I didn't know where to stay. "I could stay with Aunt Tess again maybe, but I don't know her phone number. I might be able to go to my grandmother's, but I don't know her phone number either."

"How old are you, Tommy?"

I told her.

"You shouldn't be on your own like this. You really shouldn't. You're a kid—you should be in school." Marta told me I could stay with her temporarily until I could contact one of my relatives, somewhere where I could stay permanently. I could take the train straight to Misery, she said. She'd even wire the money to me. She said she wasn't doing anything important anyway. "I'd be glad to help," she said.

I don't think someone was watching out for me, but I do think I was lucky. My grandmother always said I was born lucky, and that luck is something you either have or don't have. Up until this point in my life, I wasn't sure I believed that. The one-armed man helped me get the money from the wire and buy a ticket, and the next thing I knew I was back on the train, heading all the way to Misery.

Misery was not a bad place. It was a big small town surrounded by soybean fields. The streets were wide. The stoplights swayed in the ever-present wind. The sky was a distant sheet of blue. Most of the women in town worked for the phone company, and the men were farmers or worked for the big bank. Marta was a waitress for a hamburger joint called Beefies. She made seventy or eighty dollars a day and paid forty dollars a night to stay at the Dirge Motel. Marta spent twenty dollars on food per day, even when I stayed with her, and she saved the other twenty. "Saving is next to brushing your teeth," Marta said. "Gotta do it or you'll be sorry." For dinner I usually ate leftover hamburgers and fries.

Right from the beginning Marta called me "son." She said she wanted to call me son so nobody would think ill of her. She also said she'd always wanted a child. In retrospect she had good reason to be concerned. For whatever reason, Marta was a woman who other women seemed to dislike, especially the other waitresses at Beefies.

The first two days in Misery I stayed in the motel, coloring in coloring books on the floor. The best thing about the Dirge Motel was the plush white carpeting—it reminded me of polar bear fur. When Marta wasn't working she'd play hangman with me. When we got bored of hangman she'd play hide n' seek in the halls and lobby. When we got bored with hide n' seek we'd play tag. I wished Marta was my real aunt. Marta was like a big kid.

But when Marta took me to Beefie's she was different. Her posture stiffened, and she talked in yes-sirs and no-sirs. She introduced me to Gilda and Rhonda and Maude. I had a difficult time telling them apart at first. Gilda and Rhonda were twin sisters, both robust and with high-pitched voices. They usually wore wide striped blouses. The only real difference between them was Gilda had a gap between her two front teeth. I would always get them to talk first—that way I knew if it was Gilda or Rhonda. Maude was a seventeen-year-old runaway. She had a red scar on her arm and she had the saddest eyes I had ever seen.

"This is my son, Tommy," Marta said. I tried not to let her lie register in my eyes.

When Gilda asked Marta about me she said she got a lawyer. She said that she shared joint custody with her ex-husband. Marta could think on her feet.

"And where is he?" Gilda asked.

"You know—out east. He's a roamer."

Gilda squinted when Marta went in back to change. Then her and Rhonda whispered. I could see meanness glitter in their eyes.

Maude stood behind the register taking orders and collecting money. Her eyes bored through the walls to some distant horizon.

When Beefies wasn't busy, the manager, Mrs. Cloud, let me sit on the counter near the register. I liked this because I could talk to Maude. Maude would sing to me. Old jazz standards. Something in me needed to hear songs then, and Maude sang so softly, nobody else in the world could hear.

Marta took good care of me. She would tuck me into bed. She would treat me to ice cream now and then. She would take me to bars and dance with me to rock and roll. She didn't care if I smoked a cigarette or drank half a beer.

Still, I wondered why Marta cared. I didn't know exactly what she had at stake in me. She told me she was lonely, that she was bored, but she didn't say a thing about her own past. Marta didn't want to talk about herself. If I wanted to hear a story it would have to be about someone else. I thought this was odd.

Maude was my first real crush. Since I wasn't in school, I had plenty of time and energy to think. When I wasn't at Beefies, I'd race up and down the halls of the Dirge Motel. The maids didn't mind. When I got tired of this I'd call Maude. She lived on the other side of town.

Maude called me "kiddo," which was fine with me. She acted as if I were her little brother. Maude said she wanted to live in a world without money. I thought it was an odd thing to say.

"I hate money," she said. "What's so great about it?"

I didn't know how to answer that one.

"I saw this documentary once," she said. "It was in science class or something. Anyway, the documentary was about this tribe that wanders around the desert in Africa living on insects and roots and things. They don't have any money and they don't have any cars and things. They laugh a lot though. They laughed more than anyone I know."

Maude told me she wasn't going to college because her parents were obsessed with "a good college." They kept telling Maude she needed to fill out more applications, to raise her SAT scores. Maude told me she was going to be stubborn.

"What I want to do," she said, "you don't need a college degree for." So I asked her.

"I want to work in a junkyard. One man's trash is another man's treasure. I'd even *live* in the junkyard."

Then Maude would sing for me. "For you kiddo, I'd do anything."

Marta told me she was glad I was friends with Maude. She said it made her feel better about the universe.

Gilda and Rhonda had stopped speaking to Marta. Marta said she wasn't sure why exactly. She shrugged and said, "Some people you just can't figure out no matter what." The next time I was in Beefies, I asked Rhonda. Rhonda flipped her permed hair and straightened her red hoop earring. Blue plastic hexagons dangled from each red hoop. Each hexagon was decorated with a small red circle.

"I don't trust her is all," Rhonda said. "I don't know why. But then again, she is your mom."

When I asked why she didn't trust my mother, Rhonda said Marta just wasn't worth her trust. Rhonda said people have to earn her trust, that she doesn't freely give it out. Sometimes life seems to revolve in slow circles.

I wasn't surprised when Rhonda and Gilda accused Marta of stealing from Beefie's. Luckily for Marta the manager didn't believe a word they said, and neither did the owners, but Marta quit anyway. She said it just wasn't a healthy environment anymore.

For two days Marta sat around the motel looking at her feet. Once, she even collapsed on the plush polar bear rug with me. She didn't cry or drink or pity herself. But she did take what she called a vacation—going so far as to pitch a tent in the motel room and invite me inside. She bought a CD of cricket songs and we slept in the tent, imagining we were deep in the wilderness.

When Marta got a job mowing lawns, she said I couldn't come along. It sounded hot and dirty anyway, even in the spring. Marta said she mostly mowed the lawns of office parks anyway.

"It's not exciting."

Even though Marta no longer worked at Beefies, I still went there almost every day. For one thing, they fed me for free. I'm not sure if the management felt guilty or what, but they treated me as if Marta still worked there. Even Gilda and Rhonda patted my head, or at least they did when I didn't duck out of the way.

But I was there to see Maude. Maude said she always wanted a kid brother. As an only child Maude said she felt like a piece of meat between two tigers. She just wished her parents didn't wring their hands so much over her future.

"There are plenty of kids in the world," Maude said.

I began taking Maude over to the Dirge Motel. The motel didn't have a swimming pool or a hot tub, but we could amuse ourselves looking for quarters under the vending machines or knocking on doors and running down the hall.

I never asked to see Maude naked, but since we were bored she said why not. We went back to Martha's room and turned on the television. We were eating peanut butter straight from the jar when Maude caught a glimpse of herself in the small mirror above the sitting chair.

"Do you think I'm pretty?" Maude asked.

"I don't know," I said. I didn't think much about it. I hadn't even hit puberty yet.

"You don't know? What kind of kid brother are you?"

I really wasn't sure.

"Yes, you're pretty," I said. I felt ready for a nap. I was also starting to get restless. I wanted to go to school. Maude let me read from her chemistry book, but I didn't understand a word. I wanted to be around kids my own age.

"You really think so?" she asked. Her eyes were exposed and vulnerable-looking in the television glow.

"Yeah," I said.

She asked me what made me think she was pretty, and I said "her face." Her hair. Her sad eyes.

This is when Maude asked if I wanted to kiss her. She didn't ask if I had ever kissed a girl. She could tell I hadn't.

"Okay," I said. Maude pulled me closer on the bed, crossing her legs in front of her. She wore a dark green shirt the color of pine needles and a silver necklace adorned with a silver monkey head. She closed her eyes and opened her mouth slightly, then she pulled me toward her.

"Kiss me."

When I did, Maude pressed her tongue into mine. It felt like I was licking a slug, and I shook my head and wiped my mouth with the back of my arm. Maude opened her eyes and crossed her arms and suddenly laughed.

"Weird huh?" she said.

Then she told me she wanted me to see her boobs. Underneath her shirt she undid her bra straps. Then she lifted her shirt. When Maude asked me to touch them I did. I pressed my hand onto the right one and didn't know what to do. I just held my hand there and I felt Maude's heartbeat. It slowed. We kissed some more and she held me close.

I could have stayed in Misery for quite some time except for Randy. Randy was a man who worked with Marta. Mowing lawns. He drove those large lawnmowers you see on the side of the highway. Randy wasn't afraid of grunt work, and he wasn't intimidated by anything in this world.

Sometimes people fit expectations, and Randy fell into this category. He was short and squat with big knobby red hands and calves the size of pine logs. He wore shorts all the time—even in the snow. He never got cold.

It only took a month for Randy to ask Marta to move in with him. He lived in a house on the outskirts of town, next to a waterfall. His house was old and small and the plaster was cracked, but it was a beautiful spot. Whenever the sun was out Randy could see a rainbow from his kitchen.

Well, when Marta agreed to move in with Randy, Maude told me I should try to find another aunt to live with. Marta told me the same.

"I'm out of aunts though," I said. But then I remembered I did actually have one more—my Aunt Beth.

Maude didn't want me to leave Misery. She was looking into working for a junkyard and she was ready to share that world with me. Instead, Maude let me make phone calls from her parents' house. It took one call to my grandmother to discover where Aunt Beth lived and how to find her.

Before I left Misery Marta and Maude threw me a goodbye party at Beefie's.

Everyone was at the party. I ate hamburger after hamburger, watching myself in the shiny eyes of adults.

Bear Lake Island

I had never been on a boat. The man at the train station said that was the only way I could get to Bear Lake Island set smack in the middle of the glacial lake. I tried to phone Aunt Beth, but Gaga had warned me she didn't much like technology and rarely answered her phone. I did know where she lived. I knew that much.

Marta gave me barely enough money to purchase a train ticket and eat. I hoped ten dollars was enough to get me to Aunt Beth. I was fortunate the boat ride cost $8.99—I had enough to give a handful of change to Willie, the boatman.

But first: the water. Ever since Uncle Rusty showed me the creek, I had been entranced by the idea of water, of experiencing it. Up until that point, however, I had only watched it. I had never floated on it. As Willie handed me my life preserver, and situated me in the seat next to him, I became fixated on what lay underneath: the play of sunshine on the ripples, the never-ending movement, the reflection of trees and clouds and birds and everything above. It was as if I was entering another world—and in many ways I was.

"Young sir, like my boat?" Willie asked

"Huh?" I said, snapped from my reverie.

"My boat. What do you think?"

Since it was the first real boat I had ever seen in person—much less set foot upon—I thought it was amazing, and I told him so. In retrospect, it was nothing more than a cheap aluminum fishing boat equipped with a six horsepower engine. It did the trick though.

During the twenty-minute ride from the shore to the island in the middle of the lake, Willie wanted to hear every detail—where I had been, what I had done, who I had seen. The ride was a tug of war in this way, since I was most interested in looking at the scenery and forgetting myself, and he was most interested in me and my stories and forgetting the scenery. I told him enough to pique his interest though. I was hypnotized by the water, by the expanse of it, by its breadth.

"I'll have to come back this way to hear the rest of your stories, young sir."

Willie guided the boat with assurance, as if he had taken this route countless times. He smelled as if he were waterlogged, immersed in algae and wet rope and fish scales.

"What is she like?"

"Who's that, young sir?"

"My Aunt Beth."

Willie looked at me first, then smiled.

"A mystery to me," he said. "All the times I've been around this island, this is about the first time I'm docking on it. You know they own the whole thing, don't you?"

"No, really?"

"All I can say from folks who have been there—she likes to keep to herself. It's a whole different world there. You tell me when you come back, hear?"

Willie's boat docked at the small, almost imperceptible pier jutting into the lake. He handed me my bags and I gave him all the money I had in the world. In a way I felt free. I could see the wooden house above me. A shell path led up to the house. The path was lined with pine trees. I watched Willie's boat churn away, the water, the light in it, the ripples slapping the pier I stood upon.

As I walked up the path through the shade provided by the pine bowers, I could see the house on the hill was round. It was a circular house, made of pine, in the midst of pine, on Bear Lake Island, surrounded by water. The view from the hill was water—all glittering water.

I reached the door and knocked, bags in hand. I felt woozy. The scent of pine was almost overwhelming. No answer: I knocked again. No answer. So I sat and waited. This was not unusual. I had, by this point, developed patience. Five hours later, I was still stooped on the porch half-asleep, dozed off in the shadows.

I felt the caresses before I heard them, fingers lightly smoothing my head. I heard whispers, then felt more soft touches.

"Hey there." A voice. I opened my eyes and I was surrounded by faces—a man, a woman, four children. Their faces were soft, open, yet cloaked in the same shadows in which I dozed. I closed my eyes and opened them again. My mouth even tasted of pine.

"I'm Tommy," I said. "Beth's nephew."

The woman leaned toward me and kissed me on the forehead. She smelled different—of flowers and bread and honey, not pine, not fish.

"I've been expecting you," she said. She held out her hand and lifted me, and the children took my bags and carried them and we entered the house and she directed me to the table, also made of pine, speckled with large black knots. I immediately felt an urge to touch the knots.

"Would you like tea?"

I said I would, and Aunt Beth boiled it, and her husband—who I would come to know as Uncle Rex—led their children past us and through two large doors which they closed behind them.

"You must be exhausted," she said. "I hope you haven't waited long."

"Not too long," I lied.

She smiled at me—a luminous smile unlike any I'd ever seen. Her teeth caught the light, and her eyes seemed to open and speak. She had an expansive mouth as well: Aunt Beth was a tall, robust woman, reminding me later of a Scandinavian housewife—thick arms and ankles and neck. She kept her hair up in a bun, tied within itself. I could see why Willie described her as mysterious: Aunt Beth seemed to glow. I didn't witness a hint of pain or suffering in her face—no worry lines, no pinched folds of skin. Her face was as pure and simple as I'd ever seen in an adult.

"You rest now," she said. And I did. I let my shoulders drop, my muscles loosen.

She brought me the steaming tea and I drank it and fell asleep right there at the table. I felt my body lifted and then put to rest. I was in bed in the house surrounded by water.

Soon I was part of the family. It was perfect, Edenic really.

Aunt Beth spoiled me rotten. Whatever it was I wanted she found a way to produce. If I had a hankering for roast chicken, I had chicken. If I wanted a toy train set, the next day it was circling my bed. If I wanted a puppy, soon enough it was panting at my feet. I never truly knew how she did it, especially since we lived on an island in the middle of a lake. I never saw or heard a boat leave the island.

At the time I explained this away: the round house was expansive enough; perhaps it could store a limitless supply of food and toys and pets. I wasn't even sure how she possessed money—nobody in the family seemed to work. Ultimately it didn't matter. The result was that Aunt Beth provided; I accepted.

Her husband, Rex, was thin and ruddy-faced and bearded, his hair the color of sandpaper. He doted on her. They held hands and walked arm in arm. They stared at each other longingly across the dinner table.

Aunt Beth's children—two girls and two boys—were almost a unit to me. Katherine and Bill and Kaitlin and Bryan. They were each two years apart. The symmetry was impressive—as if they each represented a pillar stabilizing the corner of their house (if circles had corners).

In fact, when I think about Aunt Beth and the time I spent with them, "placid" is the word that comes to mind. After all I had been through I was, for once, at peace.

It may sound as if my time was uneventful there. Quite the opposite—it was filled with events. The events, however, were simply a matter of various activities I enjoyed doing. Aunt Beth took me swimming in the lagoon, showed me the underwater cave. Katherine and Bill took me hiking around the island. Uncle Rex took me fishing. This was the respite of my childhood.

After several months I realized I could easily, happily live and die on Aunt Beth's island in the middle of Bear Lake.

I remember sitting on the open-air back porch with the family after dinner one night, three or four months after I had arrived. We had a delicious supper of corn and potatoes and pork chops. Torches were aglow on each corner of the porch. The night was balmy and sweet (funny, I barely remember it raining during my time on the island). It was perfect. Everything was. I was far away from Chelsea and the desert and the hard times.

Then I thought about school. It was probably early September then.

"Where do you go to school?" I asked Kaitlin.

She blinked at me.

"School? What's school?"

I tried to explain math and history and art class and writing. I told her about the different schools I went to, how at Chelsea's I had to teach myself.

"We learn from nature here," Uncle Rex said. He jabbed at his teeth with a flat toothpick. "Corn," he said.

"Oh," I said. I didn't understand how nature could teach his children about math.

"You never heard of Pythagoras?"

Sounded familiar. I thought I recalled something about circles or rectangles. I shrugged.

"He said anything worth learning you could learn from observing the world around you."

I didn't know what to say, so I kept my mouth closed.

As if to prove his point, Uncle Rex took me out into the woods the next day. In retrospect, I think he may have been angry at me for questioning some aspect of their lives, but at the time I thought it was just another fun outing. I don't remember learning algebra from the trees and rocks.

As the weather became colder and drier, I grew restless for knowledge, for expanding my mind. The house and land and water were beautiful, but I felt as if my brain was slowly moldering. So I asked Aunt Beth for some books—she had never disappointed before.

She raised her eyebrows at me and looked away.

"Now why would you want dusty old books? Rex didn't take you out into the woods?"

I can't exactly remember how I put it (I was only twelve), but I believe I told her I had to learn and that if I didn't learn something I wouldn't like myself, that school was why I had to leave Gaga's house to begin with. I had made an investment. I realize these are atypical kid things to say, but it's what I said. Or something close.

"You can relax, Tommy," she said. "You don't ever need to leave us. You are a part of us."

It was at that moment, for me, that the gig was up. What seemed perfect immediately felt like a perfect trap. Where Aunt Beth was Santa Claus early on, she had, in my mind, transformed herself into Stalin—no new knowledge, no outside input, no exposure to anything other than trees. No contact with the outside world either—not even letters. I'm still not sure how she knew I was coming. In retrospect I guess she just said that to make me feel unwelcome, even if she was caught off-guard.

I don't like tearing a relative down, much less a family. However, once I realized the family unit on Bear Island was based on the principle of self-isolation, I knew I had to leave as soon as I could. I had lived that before. Didn't want it again.

In a sense my time with Aunt Beth wasn't that different than my time with Gaga—they both lived on islands of a sort. Aunt Beth was like her mother—she distrusted authority, and technology, and would rather be left to her own devices. The difference, however, was that where Gaga was tough and severe and hard-nosed, Beth made me always feel at home. This was the danger.

Still, I quickly realized I needed to take action if I wanted to have a normal life. It was at this point I felt the greatest desire to find my parents, to at least speak with them. I had grown weary of shuttling from relative to relative and I was ready for one home—somewhere, anywhere. And if not my parents, Gaga was an acceptable alternative.

In retrospect I wish I wasn't such a "good boy." Aunt Beth had a boat; I could have easily rowed it off in the middle of the night. But I was afraid—of the boat, of the water, of floating endlessly. Aunt Beth had only just instructed me how to swim; I flailed about like a cat in a bathtub. I loved watching the water, but in it I was helpless.

Instead, I considered Willie my way out. My only problem—I had no idea how to contact him. I began hoarding bottles. Every day, at some languorous time when the others were busy or distracted, I would walk down the shell path to the lake and toss a bottle into the water, as far out as I could throw it. My messages would read something like:

Willie—
This is young sir, on the island. <u>Please</u> come get me. I would like to go home now. Away from this island. Please!
Young Sir

I did this for two months—every day. There must still be bottles floating around Bear Lake Island. In December I walked down to the water one day to find a bottle on the pier, sitting there glimmering in the early morning light. Inside it was a note I still have.

"Young Sir—
Message received. Will be here for you tomorrow morning. 5:00.
Willie."

My stomach tightened, knowing I would soon be on my way. I ran up the shell path into the house (Beth and Rex were just waking up) and began packing my belongings right away. Subtlety was not my strong suit. I didn't care. I wanted to return to the world. On the island I felt ensnared by beauty, seduced by the splendor of water.

During my last full day on the island I took a walk with Aunt Beth around the perimeter—about two miles.

"I used to do this all the time," she said, making a circle with her index finger. "It relaxes me."

I was only a kid, but I sensed that somehow she knew. I wasn't sure if Willie contacted her as well, or if she read one of my notes, or if she just had an inkling.

"It's a nice island," I said.

Beth's family had built a path running completely around the island, cutting through the pines, the scrub, rising along the bluffs overlooking the lake. We walked, sipping apple juice from a canteen we shared.

"Do you feel like I'm secretive?" she asked me.

I didn't say anything at first—just kept walking. I drank some apple juice and screwed the canteen closed.

"No," I lied.

"My children feel I am," she said, looking straight ahead. We passed under a shady area into the dappled sunshine. The trees loomed. "You understand why: you lived with my mother."

I asked if her children had ever met Gaga. She shook her head. I remember Beth wore a turquoise necklace that day. The color of it reminded me of my Aunt Chelsea for some reason. I thought about Beth's children growing up to rebel against her. I imagined Bill as a leather-clad biker, Katherine in some dilapidated urban warehouse. Maybe not. Maybe her four children would live in nearby towns, working as small-town teachers or lawyers, visiting Beth on weekends. I didn't think so.

"Maybe Gaga could visit here." As soon as I said it I realized how ridiculous it sounded. Gaga would never travel if she could help it.

We hiked up the bluff at the far end of the island and stood there looking out over the lake. The view was all glimmering water and trees—not a single occupancy in sight. I wondered if Beth was lonely—no friends, just family. Surrounded by nature in the middle of a lake. I watched geese lift themselves from the lake, ascend into the air. I watched them soar above the trees and into the sky beyond, disappearing into the horizon.

"Pretty soon they will be grown," Beth said. "Then I won't be able to spoil them any longer."

"Me too," I said.

"You too."

The next morning Willie was at the pier, engine idling. He shook my hands fervently, patted my back. I tossed my bags into the back of the boat, and he turned the boat toward the shore.

Willie didn't ask questions, which was perfect. I didn't feel like talking.

On the table where I ate with Aunt Beth and her family I left a note. I can't remember exactly what it said—but it thanked them for allowing me to stay and said I was heading to Gaga's and that I'm sure Gaga would love to see them at some point. I mentioned that I had to go to school, that I felt it was something I needed to continue, and I did.

As Willie's boat cut through the water, however, I didn't think of Beth or the note or the island at all. I watched the water part for us, over and over the curtains of water parting.

The End

The End?

Endings are a kind of death, a controlled death—a death in the sense that he or she who tells a story, who renders it alive, also must fix in the reader the essential meaning of the story. The end is the end of meaning, the end of our own exploration. How do we explain?

As a young boy, Gaga didn't tell me many stories, but when she did she was *generous*. She would say, "Tommy, now you choose how you want it to end." This is your story, she implied. I'm just *telling* it. You tell me how you want it to end.

You've followed my story this far. Now you may choose:

1

But we never made it to Gaga's.

Willie and I stopped at a grubby pay phone to call ahead, but this is when we heard news that Gaga was no longer with us. Later I found out she had been dead for days before one of the neighbors stumbled upon her—Gaga was supposed to drive Mrs. Thornhill down to the valley.

Willie was a gentle man in his own particular formal way.

"I'm sorry, young sir. I'm so sorry."

I watched Willie drift toward me and then sit on the curb next to me. Weeds surrounding us.

Willie's legs seemed to sway beneath him. I wondered then how often he was on the boat on Bear Lake. How many hours did he spend on land anymore? If a man can have sea legs can one also have lake legs?

"It's fine," I said. I admit it: I was fighting off the tears. I kept thinking of Gaga looming over me, scolding me for a job half-done.

This was her. She was consummately her, more herself than anyone I know.

He told me about his own grandmother, who he barely knew. "A thin little wisp of a lady she was, hardly there. I almost imagine the wind blowing her away. Like the seeds of a dandelion, young sir." He said she was still young when she passed on. His other grandparents he didn't know at all.

"What do I do now?"

We talked about it. Willie was inclined to bring me right back to Bear Island, but I didn't want that—there was no going back. For the same reason I couldn't return to any of my other aunts. I was bent on being self-sufficient—self-sufficient enough, at least, to make do without going backwards. I was also very, very stubborn.

"You can stay with me, young sir. It is just me."

"No," I said. "I can't do that to you. You have enough."

He protested, saying that he'd love my company. But it was out of the question.

"I'm sure there must be a place for orphans somewhere."

"No, young sir. You do not want to stay there," Willie said. "Those are not good places. Dangerous."

"That's exactly where I want to go then. That's what I deserve."

Willie didn't like it but I let him drive me until we found one. Many times he asked me if I knew what I was doing. I never said I did, but I also wasn't backing down. Gaga was her own person. I would be my own. At least this was my thinking at the time.

After a day of searching we found an orphanage a mile or two off the highway in a leafy town surrounded by gardens and parks.

As we pulled up to the low-lying building I was struck by the scent of roses—plush rose bushes lined the walk.

"I'll take the risk. Just drop me here, Willie," I said.

"But young sir," he said. "What if they can't take you?"

"Then I'll convince them," I said.

"You know best," he said.

When he waved goodbye I could see his fingers were crossed.

I could lie and say I fit right in. I could pretend to have enjoyed my stay at the Willard Boy's Orphanage. At certain moments, both of these statements were true. As a generalization, however, neither were.

The Willard Boy's Orphanage was nothing like the orphanage of the popular imagination. No porridge. No huddled grimy children in rags. No stern beefy matrons whipping boys with yard sticks and locking them in the broom closet.

Instead, most of the other orphans were both well-behaved and balanced. They had names like Stevens and Gus and Ed and Walter. We ate quiche and salads and penne and corn on the cob. It wasn't restaurant-quality food by any means, but then again I've hardly eaten at any restaurants. It was healthy and colorful.

In many ways life at the Willard Boy's Orphanage was a return to the kind of domestic stability Gaga provided. We all helped with the garden. We washed the deck and sidewalk. We organized the paperbacks in the library. There were only twenty-three of us, but we accomplished plenty. And we felt a sense of satisfaction. We had good days and bad days, but in many ways the orphanage was an *improvement*.

Even Mr. Harrison, the "manager" of the orphanage, offered a steady diet of praise and moral support. He was an ex-
teacher who was absolutely comfortable with children and knew
how to be both firm, and at the same time, vaguely paternal and
hopeful.

We never talked of adoption. It was taboo to even mention
the word.

At night I bunked with a kid two years older than me by the
name of Jacob Quint. Jacob lost his parents in a fire—or so the
rumor went—and like me, he didn't have ready or willing relatives to pick up the slack. There was, as a result, a melancholy
cloud which hung over him. In his sleep he would moan or cry
softly, though we never asked about it and he never volunteered.

The Willard Boy's Orphanage was very good to me, and
though I've lost touch with many of my comrades by now, I am
still in touch with a few. At age eighteen we were actively en-
couraged to seek employment or attend college—just like teen-
agers in the so-called real world. The rule was we could stay on
at the orphanage six months after eighteen, but at that point we
would be effectively forced out.

Well, I lucked out.

When I turned eighteen Mr. Harrison invited me into his
office.

"Sit down, Tommy."

I did. I remember watching his cowlick blow in the breeze
from the window.

He offered me a hard candy from his blue bowl—it was
a kind of Willard staple. I took a butterscotch, unwrapping it
quickly.

"You seem to like it here," he said.

"Sure, I do," I said. "You know it."

"You're comfortable?" he said.

I nodded.

"Well, I'd like to make you an offer," he said.

I would be his assistant, essentially. Minimal pay, but room and board would be free and when he decided to leave, if I did a good job, I'd be next in line to potentially take over. At least I'd probably get an interview.

Sometimes all you need in life is one person to see the potential in you.

For me it made all the difference. I'm sleeping tonight in the same room I slept in when I first arrived.

I'm Mr. Harrison now.

I guide with a steady hand. I guide with many behind me. I stare straight ahead when I walk and only blink when I need to.

OR 2

My mother stood over me. I didn't know where I was; I hardly knew who I was. How did I know this was my mother? How does a flower know the sun?

Her face spread before me—a half-smile, a concerned wrinkle, eyes open wide and peering down on me. She touched my head and I watched the hand slowly descend from light to the shadow beneath her.

"Hey there, kiddo," she whispered. "If you turn over I can pat your back."

I did as she said and closed my eyes.

The breeze washed over my face and through my hair. I felt her hand caress me, patting my small form as my breath deepened and grew.

"Relax," she whispered. "It will be over soon."

At this point I realized where I was—surrounded by whitewhitewhite walls. White light. White sheets. White bed. I closed my eyes again and just let it happen.

"It's not your fault, Tommy," she said. "You've had rotten luck. But such is life. I'm sure I don't need to tell you this."

I remember lying there, allowing my mother to pat circles on my back. At the same time I wanted so badly to ask her questions. I wanted to know who she was. I wanted to know where she'd lived for the past decade. I wanted to know if she'd thought of me, if she'd ever wondered where I was. Maybe these questions would all lead to easily formulated answers. Maybe they wouldn't.

I felt the crinkly thin sheets beneath me and just then became aware of the bleeping and blipping machinery in the room.

"Shhhh," she said, still rubbing my back. "Relax. You rest."

I must have; the next thing I knew I was asleep.

When I awoke she was gone. I was in a larger room with more machines. There was the doctor, nurses flanking him.

"There has been an accident," he said. "But you are in good hands here. We do need to do some tests though."

I nodded.

"You will feel a numbness descend on you. First you will breathe in and it will taste a bit funny, but then soon enough you will be asleep then awake again. Don't you worry."

"Where is my mother?"

"Don't you worry," he said again.

And then the mask descended.

When I awoke I didn't have hands. I screamed and screamed until the nurses came and the doctors held me down and then the mask descended again.

When I awoke again I didn't have hands or feet. My limbs just ended with a rounded nub. My mouth was bandaged shut and I was lashed to the bed.

My mother came and she patted my stomach as I looked up to her for help.

"It had to be done, son," she said. "You have to trust me. If they didn't remove your extremities the disease would have gone all the way to your heart and lungs and that would've been it."

I was so utterly shaken and distraught. I wanted Gaga. I wondered what happened to Willie. I didn't know if I could trust this woman in front of me. Perhaps she was my mother. Perhaps she wasn't. Perhaps I could no longer trust my instincts. She patted me for hours though and she appeared to be my mother. She felt like my mother. How could I know one way or another? I was in epistemological crises. Worse, I couldn't move to investigate.

For days it went on like this. For days I zoned in and out. I wasn't in pain, or at least I don't remember pain (so perhaps my memory is suppressing it).

Then, suddenly, clarity: I was alert.

The sun shone. I was basked in it. My mouth was free.

My mother fed me mashed potatoes. I could only lean forward or backward, side to side. I arched my neck like a turtle straining for food.

"What has happened to me?"

"Don't you worry, Tommy," she said. She wore a turquoise

necklace, which dangled into the form of a U under her neck. The color was an intense turquoise. I don't know that I've ever seen a brighter color.

"I don't have hands or feet. I'm scared," I said.

And this was as honest and direct as I could put it.

"It's going to be okay. They aren't done yet."

A fan spun overhead.

I felt nauseous.

She held my arm, her fingers wrapped around the nub.

She looked younger than I would've thought.

I wondered what happened to her.

Where was my father?

What happened to my feet and toes?

What accident?

My thoughts whirled at twice the rate of the fan blades.

Was I dreaming this?

I couldn't feel my body. The strangest feeling.

I woke up with wheels for feet and pincers for hands.

The doctors told me this was the best they could do, given the rarity of my condition, and their fear of contamination.

My mother came in and held my right pincers.

She stroked my head.

"We've all missed you," she said. "Let's go home."

"Home?" I said. "Where is home?"

"You are still out of it, aren't you?"

She drove us a short way—maybe twenty minutes—to a suburban enclave.

She rolled me up the sidewalk—my legs were wobbly, as if on rollerblades. Nothing hurt. And I can't recall anything.

Inside was my room, as if I never left, as if I was always there—my things, my bed, everything.

A sign reading "Welcome Home" in rainbow colors above my bed.

And I was home. A new start.

OR 3

It was only a matter of days between the time Willie dropped me off reeling from the rocky boat-ride escapade to the time when I was sitting back at Gaga's kitchen table, chopping apples again. The days returned to a rhythm I was used to. I knew the scents, the chores, the sounds. At first glance nothing had changed.

Still. After a handful of days I knew this was a slightly different version of Gaga. She seemed more remote, as if some part of her had become displaced in the years since she raised me.

"I am getting old, Thomas. This is true," she said. "I am not sickly, mind you. I just can't quite do the things I once did. I ache."

I knew then I'd have to take care of her. It was fine by me at that point. I would trade an extra dose of work for stability.

I could also see that she had softened a bit, or perhaps I had hardened. Perspective is interesting that way.

We agreed that since I would attempt to attend school my chores would be limited to one hour in the afternoon. "Agreed" was the new Gaga. The old Gaga would just bark orders, direct.

The new Gaga was willing to accommodate. She was too tired to bark.

I can handle this, I thought.

When school started in September Gaga arranged for one of the "neighbors" to drive me down the mountain to school. Mrs. Crews lived on the south side of Pike's Peak, so it was a complete act of generosity for her to pick me up. She could just as easily have driven around the mountain on Backlick Road. I suspected Gaga agreed to pay for gas, but I found out later this wasn't so. Mrs. Crews looked out for Gaga.

Mrs. Crews had a son, Jimmy, who played linebacker for the football team. Our school only had two hundred and ninety eight students—any tall or portly kid became a lineman. Some were girls. Jimmy liked to memorize facts in the car.

"I'm not that smart," he said. "So I gotta work hard."

He carried around a black aluminum box of index cards. The index cards were sorted by color—each color represented a different field of study. Red for history. Blue for math. Yellow for English. As his mother wound down the mountain, Jimmy would hand me a stack and ask me to quiz him. So I would.

Jimmy ended up class valedictorian.

The first time I set eyes on Tammy I thought she was incredibly annoying. We were in "homeroom" together, which nobody took seriously, of course. It was just an excuse to keep us in school for a longer period of time—or at least this is what we suspected. It was only twenty minutes, and most of the students used it either as a time to do the homework they forgot to do the night before or to flirt with someone else in class.

Tammy was a good student, so she was in the second category. Tammy was tall and lanky with frizzy brown hair to her shoulders. She had a small, almost triangular gap between her front teeth, and thin lips that spread along her face when she smiled—which was often. She had this way or arching her eyebrows when she talked, however, that irked me to no end. It always seemed as if she thought she knew more than everyone else. In a sense, she did. Where Jimmy was an expert memorizer, Tammy actually knew more than most of our teachers—and she often corrected them blithely. In history, Mrs. Heinlen would misstate some minor fact about the Revolutionary War and Tammy would raise her hand: "Excuse me, Mrs. Heinlen, I think that was in December, 1777, not January, 1778."

But in homeroom it was a different matter altogether. Tammy fixed her attention on me from the get-go.

"Tommy Twice," she said. "That's precious." She liked "precious."

"That's my name," I said.

"Wouldn't it be cuter than cute if we were a couple—Tommy and Tammy. All that alliteration."

"It would be something," I said.

I knew she just felt like impressing me by saying "alliteration."

"It would be a cute something," Tammy said, her hand on my thigh.

Up to this point I had little, if any, experience with girls. There were, obviously, girls in my classes when I was with Aunt

Penny, but nobody stood out in particular. My contact with the female gender was limited if not downright pathetic. Or this was my perception at least. So I didn't know that a hand on the thigh could be a come on, a sign. I thought it was just Tammy being Tammy.

So when Tammy French-kissed me on the running track, I thought this was just her way of saying "hi." In a way it was.

Tammy was also the quarterback of our football team. She had a strong right arm that so impressed the coach he never used another quarterback until Tammy graduated.

On the sidelines he said, "That tomboy can throw, can't she?" He was right.

During the games I would cheer on the team, and Tammy in particular, of course. She would take off her helmet, bounce over to me and stick her tongue down my throat.

"Hiya, Tommy," she'd say, grinning her gap-toothed smile.

That's right: I was dating the quarterback.

Certain paradoxical facts never cease to amaze me: love and hate dance in counterpoint; with time, what once seemed immense seems inconsequential; change is ceaseless yet often invisible.

I was a boy who found myself suddenly immersed in something he didn't quite understand. My analytical mind didn't know how to process what my senses and body experienced. All I knew was Tammy seemed to tap into to some part of my being which I didn't previously know existed. This was enough. On the strength of this the years blurred.

Next thing I knew my wife—not Tammy, though she set me on this path—was sitting next to me at our kitchen table at the bottom of the mountain, rings on our fingers. A contented life as a result of choices, perhaps a dumb life. Children. The whole American dream of settling down and becoming ordinary.

That's me now: ordinary. Settled. Perhaps tapped out. End of story.

Today I take my children to Tai Kwan Do, then to a birthday party, then drive to the nursery to purchase a dogwood for the backyard—there's a gap where we cut down the diseased spruce. Karen and I plant the dogwood, eat lunch, then go to Home Depot to check out the ceramic tile choices for the hall half-bath. We'll likely, however, end up going with marble. It's a different world.

Karen has heard it all before. My kids love it when I tell these stories, however. For you, this is all new.

One day several years ago, Jacob, my son, came home from school with a wall-sized map of the United States. He pinned it to his bedroom wall with red and yellow stick pins. That night Jacob asked me to point to the places I'd been as a child. I couldn't do it.

"I'm not sure," I said.

"What do you mean?"

"I never was exactly sure where I was," I explained. "Can't help it."

"Really?"

"Yes," I said. "Everything was different then. Go to sleep now. We have a long day tomorrow."

As I stood up, I looked at the dots on the map. I am one of those, I knew. That's all.

OR 4

I'm not unhappy; I'm not. I live my life just like anyone else. The creek is plentiful—usually is. Crawfish are regularly dependable and not too difficult to catch (I have experience now). Unlike many others around here, I have a leak-proof tarp. I have enough clothes to stay warm, mostly. Food is a scramble, even with the creek. But that's the way of the world. Always has been, always will be.

Today I'm heading with Danny-boy to the "kitchens"—that's what he calls them anyway. It's three dumpsters in back of a strip mall in Talewaga. There's a Pizza Hut, a Dunkin Donuts, a Taco Bell and so forth. The dumpsters are all positioned together in a nexus of freebies.

Having been on a trip to the kitchen before, I knew the trick was to be quick and to go late. We usually bring a few extra people, a few extra black plastic bags, but tonight it's just the two of us. If we're lucky we'll get enough tossed pizza, donuts and tacos to last us three or four days.

No choice, especially in wintertime when the creek is all but frozen over.

I pretty much keep to myself these days, keeps me young. At least that's what Gilda used to tell me. She was a rare lady around these parts—dumped by her husband, trying to "reclaim herself," she said. She's been gone twelve years now, but she made an impression on me, that's for damn sure. She was sweet on me though, and any time she ran across my path she'd tell me I looked younger than my age. She probably meant I looked my age, but I understand her gist. I do take care of myself.

That said, it's tough here. Rats scurry through here every night (I sleep with a rusty knife I found in the tunnel). Fleas. Lice. Poison ivy. I usually have some combination of all of the above. In the winter I have to duck into the Shell station, but that's a forty-minute walk up Route 18 and my knees aren't what they once were.

It was a jolt, then, to see Mickey Orlean outside of my tarp one morning.

He didn't remind me at all of a clown this time; nothing garish or unbuttoned about him. Instead, he was dressed in black sweatpants and a blue parka (it was drizzly that morning).

"I found you," he said. "Tommy, you have no idea how long I've been looking for you."

It took me about fifteen minutes to realize who he was. It was as if he emerged from another life, some kind of spring chick squirming anew from a sticky-moist shell. He had to explain and my synapses don't fire like they once do. Perhaps malnutrition is to blame.

"Mickey," I said. I had forgotten almost completely my former life—my aunts, Gaga, everybody. Focusing on the day-to-day was enough to keep me occupied. Didn't have time for the past until Mickey showed up.

I invited him into my "living room." He squatted, he said, so as to not dampen his pants.

"You know how much Gaga cared for you. We all do."

I listened.

"Somehow I got the, you know, the inheritance, but you were never meant to be shut out. Nobody was. Nobody planned it the way it went. It just happened and then you were gone…"

"Yup," I said. "It did happen quickly alright. I agree."

"Do you have a bank?" Mickey said. "I mean, a place where you can…you know, cash a check."

I asked him to keep his voice down, said that others would be after him—after his money—if they heard.

"No," I said. "Look…" I told him I didn't want any handouts. I told him I'm comfortable, that this is where I landed. No mother, no father—it's okay. Not my fate, I said.

He pleaded me to take it, said his wife would never understand if I didn't accept something.

"I'd offer you a room at the house, but we're packed to the gills with the kids and all," he said.

I asked him how much he was offering.

"Ten grand," he said.

I thought hard about it and decided that what I really wanted was a weekend in a motel—a bed and a shower and a few hot meals. I told him this.

"And if you'd like you can get me some cans. I can always use beans and soup."

This is what happened. Mickey drove me to the nicest motel around and I checked in. The guy behind the counter eyed me, but Mickey was there and he paid for it in full. Then he gave me a few hundred from his wallet for food.

"I have to get back for dinner," he said. "You know, the family and everything. But there's an Italian place right over there and a steakhouse and other things next to it. I'll be back on Sunday evening to get you."

I had the best weekend of my life.

I:

—Showered until the hot water ran out. I could feel years of grime and grit and dead skin washing away.

—Ate more steak and potatoes and broccoli and baked ziti and eggplant than I'd ever seen in my life.

—Slept for twelve hours straight.

—Watched television! It took me half an hour to figure out how to turn it on with all the buttons and dials, but I did. And then I stared in amazement at the foolishness of it all.

—Turned on the heat when I was cold. And then some.

—Laughed, nestled in a mound of blankets and pillows and softness.

I didn't mind returning. I had to, I knew that. I couldn't accept Mickey's guilt money, and I didn't even consider it that.

He was just trying to help. The inner workings of family politics are beyond any understanding. It's not his fault.

I had the weekend of a lifetime (at least a recent one), a fortress of canned food, and stories to tell the guys under the bridge for weeks. What more could I want?

One moment in the sun, then back to reality. But at least I had the moment. There is always that.

OR 5

Every word I've uttered is a lie, including these. They are half-truths, at the very best.

To wit, my name is not Tommy.

To wit, I'm not an orphan.

To wit, I don't know a Gaga or a Chelsea or a Penny (good names though, all).

Perhaps I've concocted these pages to boost my own frail ego. Perhaps I recline on my tan sofa in my airy split-level with floral patterned pillows and a two-tiered coffee table made of glass and iron ($1,176 at Crate and Barrel).

However, I'm an emotional orphan (thus the half-truth). Or perhaps a metaphysical orphan. A Tommy resides in me, but now he is off the hook. Let him traverse the byways and vagaries of his relatives. Let him live a good life. Let him find happiness and a home. I have my own (at least one of them).

Then again these words are lies and half-truths, also. Perhaps all words are. What is a word? A word is an abstraction, a manifestation of our attempt to capture in language what can never completely be captured: life! You can't transcribe it.

We must live it to know. Words can only provide an impression, at best.

This is the paradox.

And such is this.

The real orphans are words, always stumbling about to capture what must be said. And here they go again.

About the Author

Nathan Leslie is the author of six books of short fiction, one book of poetry and editor of two anthologies. He was the series editor for Dzanc Books' annual *Best of the Web* anthology and is the former fiction editor of *Pedestal Magazine*. He lives in Northern Virginia, and teaches at Northern Virginia Community College.